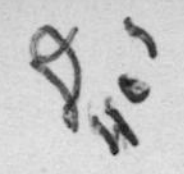

A DEADLY GAMBLE . . .

Clint topped a rise and the rider ahead of him was no longer in sight. Obviously, the man had decided to make a move. Clint had two choices. He could lay back and see how patient the man was, or he could ride forward and see what the fella had in mind. Short of being shot in the back, Clint felt sure he would be able to handle whatever the man had.

He gave Eclipse his head and started down.

Bankhead waited for the rider to go past him, then stepped out and called, "Hold it right there."

The rider stopped and froze.

"Why are you following me?"

"You mind if I turn around and see who I'm talking to?" Clint asked.

"Turn slowly," Bankhead said, "and keep your hand away from your gun."

"You're the boss, friend."

Clint turned and saw Bankhead standing there with his gun out and pointed at him. He swallowed once, realizing the man could have shot him in the back if he wanted to. But he'd taken that chance and had come out of it okay.

So far . . .

DON'T MISS THESE ALL-ACTION WESTERN SERIES FROM THE BERKLEY PUBLISHING GROUP

THE GUNSMITH by J. R. Roberts

Clint Adams was a legend among lawmen, outlaws, and ladies. They called him . . . the Gunsmith.

LONGARM by Tabor Evans

The popular long-running series about U.S. Deputy Marshal Long—his life, his loves, his fight for justice.

SLOCUM by Jake Logan

Today's longest-running action Western. John Slocum rides a deadly trail of hot blood and cold steel.

BUSHWHACKERS by B. J. Lanagan

An action-packed series by the creators of Longarm! The rousing adventures of the most brutal gang of cutthroats ever assembled—Quantrill's Raiders.

DIAMONDBACK by Guy Brewer

Dex Yancey is Diamondback, a southern gentleman turned con man when his brother cheats him out of the family fortune. Ladies love him. Gamblers hate him. But nobody pulls one over on Dex . . .

WILDGUN by Jack Hanson

Will Barlow's continuing search for his daughter, kidnapped by the Blackfeet Indians who slaughtered the rest of his family.

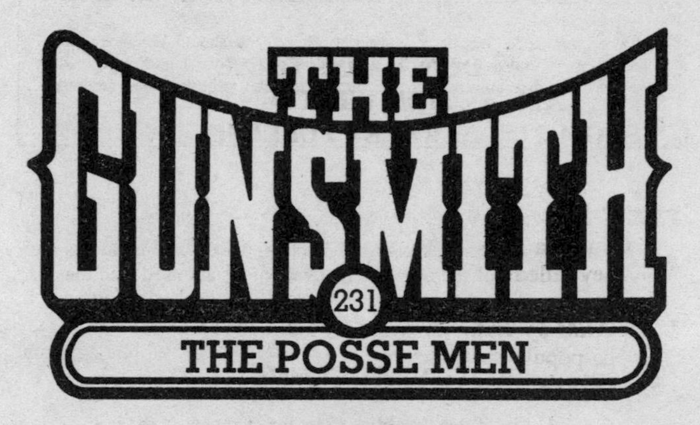

J. R. ROBERTS

JOVE BOOKS, NEW YORK

THE POSSE MEN

A Jove Book / published by arrangement with
the author

PRINTING HISTORY
Jove edition / March 2001

For information address: The Berkley Publishing Group,
a division of Penguin Putnam Inc.,
375 Hudson Street, New York, New York 10014.

The Penguin Putnam Inc. World Wide Web site address is
http://www.penguinputnam.com

ISBN: 0-515-13031-1

A JOVE BOOK®
Jove Books are published by The Berkley Publishing Group,
a division of Penguin Putnam Inc.,
375 Hudson Street, New York, New York 10014.
JOVE and the "J" design
are trademarks belonging to Penguin Putnam Inc.

PRINTED IN THE UNITED STATES OF AMERICA

10 9 8 7 6 5 4 3 2 1

ONE

It had been a long time since Clint Adams had been in Abilene—so long that, at the time, Wild Bill Hickok had been wearing a badge there. Clint had agreed to be a deputy, and things had gone terribly wrong. Hickok had been in conflict with cattlemen and saloon owners at the time, his eyesight was failing and, in one terrible moment, he had accidentally shot one of his own deputies.

Not long after that, he'd been shot and killed in Deadwood.

So Clint rode into Abilene, Kansas, determined to put its demons behind him.

He went through his usual routine when arriving in a town. Livery, hotel, something to eat, and a beer. He did it all without running into anyone he knew—which was no surprise, after all the years he'd let go by.

Abilene had not changed all that much. It had expanded, become larger, but still looked like the rough cattle town it had been last time he was there.

After the livery he got a room at the Alhambra, and ate in their dining room. That done he went into their saloon and had a beer. Once his stomach and his thirst were satisfied it was time to satisfy his curiosity about who the marshal was these days.

He left the Alhambra and walked to where he remembered the marshal's office having been. When Hickok had been Marshal there'd been a shingle outside saying J.B. HICKOK, MARSHAL. Now the hooks where the shingle had hung from were still there, but there was no shingle.

He knocked on the door and entered. Sitting behind the desk was a young man of about twenty-two or -three, wearing the badge of a deputy marshal.

"Can I help ya?" he asked eagerly.

Clint wondered if the boy qualified or if he had simply been the only one looking for the job.

"I just got into town," Clint said, "and wanted to check in with the marshal. Is he around?"

"Around town, maybe," the young deputy said, "but not around here. If you tell me your name I'll let him know you was lookin' for him."

"All right," Clint said. "My name is Clint Adams. Tell him I just got in, don't really know how long I'll be stay—"

"Wait a minute!" the boy interrupted excitedly. "Did you say you was Clint Adams?"

"That's right."

"The Gunsmith?"

Clint made a face and said, "Yes."

The deputy stood up so fast his chair fell over backward. He couldn't get around the desk fast enough and when he reached Clint he grabbed his hand and started pumping it.

"I got to tell you what a real honor it is to meet you, Mr. Adams," he said. "I know everythin' there is to know about you—well, I mean, not everythin' there is to know, but everythin' that was ever wrote about you."

"I'd think you'd have something better to do with you time, Deputy," Clint said, reclaiming his hand.

"No sir!" the deputy said. "Why . . . I got to tell you, sir, that you're my idol. Yes, sir, I decided a long time ago that I wanted to be just like you, and that's what I'm tryin'—"

"Believe me, son," Clint said, "I'm nobody you should want to be just like."

"Well, I got to argue with ya there, Mr. Adams," the deputy said.

"What's your name, son?"

"Alex," the boy said, "Deputy Marshal Alex McCord, sir . . . uh, at your service."

"Well, Deputy McCord," Clint said, "I don't want you to be at my service. I just want you to tell the marshal that I'm here."

"I'll sure do that, Mr. Adams," McCord said. "He's gonna be right excited that you're here."

"You think so?"

"I know so."

"And how's that?"

"Well . . . he talks about you all the time."

"He does?"

"Yes, sir."

"And why is that?"

"Well . . . he says he knows you."

"Is that right?"

"Yes, sir," the deputy said. "Says you and him been friends a long time, been through thick and thin together. That's what he's always sayin'—well, not always sayin'. I mean, he don't talk about you all the time, but ever since I found out about you and him bein' friends

I sort of ask him about you all the time. You know, I ask him to tell stories—"

"So the marshal says he knows me?"

"Yes, sir." Then the boy frowned. "Don't he? I mean, he ain't been lyin' ta me all this time, has he? Lord, I'd be real disappointed if the marshal's been lyin' ta me about that!"

"I can't tell you if he's been lying to you, Deputy," Clint said, "until you tell me his name."

"Well, sir, his name's—"

The boy stopped short as the door opened and the man in question, the marshal of Abilene, stepped into the office. He and Clint saw each other at the same time, and both said, "Well, I'll be . . ."

TWO

"Clint!"

"Joe Bags!"

Joe Bags had been about the deputy's age when Clint first met him, and now he was Marshal of Abilene. Clint was surprised at the tinge of pride he felt in seeing the marshal's badge on Bags's chest.

"Then you do know him!" Deputy McCord shouted, pointing at Joe Bags.

"Of course I do," Bags said. He charged Clint with his hand out and the two men shook hands.

Clint took a good look at Bags, noticing that the man had filled out with age. To the best of his recollection Bags had to be in his early thirties now.

"Goddamn," Bags said, "how many years has it been?"

"A few," Clint said. "You're looking good."

"So are you."

"How long have you been marshal of Abilene?"

"A few months," Bags said. "I see you met my deputy."

"Yes," Clint said.

"I hope he didn't gush over you too much."

"Some," Clint said. "How much is too much?"

"Let's go get a drink and catch up," Bags said, pulling Clint toward the door. He saw McCord following them and stopped. "Where are you going?"

"I'm going with you."

"You're staying here and manning the office."

"B-but—"

"You don't have any catching up to do," Bags said. "Stay here and I'll relieve you in a while."

"But—"

"Don't forget we have prisoners in the back."

That seemed to deflate the young man.

"All right."

"I won't be long, Alex," Bags said. "Come on, Clint."

Clint followed Bags outside.

"He's kind of young, isn't he?" Clint asked.

"So was I, if you remember. Anyplace in particular you want to drink?"

"It's your town," Clint said. "You pick."

"Anyplace you don't want to drink?"

"No."

"All right, then," Bags said. "The Cattleman."

"Lead the way."

Bags turned left and started walking, with Clint by his side.

The Cattleman was actually a private club, Bags explained, but of course they didn't object to the marshal drinking there.

"Or his guest," he added, as they went through the front door.

From the looks of it the Cattleman was once a large

hotel which had been taken over and turned into a private club with rooms available for members. Bags led Clint into the bar, acknowledging some greetings along the way.

"Beer?" Bags asked as they reached the bar.

"Sounds good."

"Two beers, Jake," Bags said to the bartender.

"Comin' up, Marshal."

Clint looked around and came to two conclusions. One, the club members were curious about who he was and two, he didn't think they were as happy to have their marshal among them as Joe Bags seemed to think. Not judging from the looks on their faces.

"Here ya go," Jake said, putting two cold ones down in front of them.

"Thanks, Jake." Bags picked his up and turned to face Clint. "To old friends."

Clint picked up his mug and drank to that.

"What brings you to Abilene, Clint?" Bags asked.

"I thought it was about time I came back."

"How long has it been?"

"Longer than since you and I saw each other," Clint said. "Hickok was Marshal."

"Wow," Bags said, "that is a long time. What do you think of the place?"

"A lot of it's the same," Clint said, "some different."

"No ghosts?"

"I'm hoping not."

"Well, can I convince you to stay around a while?" Bags asked. "Maybe help me whip young McCord into shape?"

"I can stay a few days."

"Maybe more? We got a lot of catching up to do."

"Maybe more," Clint said, giving in.

"Marshal?"

Both Clint and Bags turned at the sound of the voice. Clint saw a tall, barrel-chested individual with iron-gray hair and dark, jowly cheeks. It was odd, but the face looked as if it belonged on a shorter, chubbier man.

"Mr. Bahr. What can I do for you?"

"I was wondering if you'd made any progress on that matter we, uh, discussed earlier in the week?"

"I'm still working on it, Mr. Bahr," Bags said. "Let me introduce you to my friend. Clint Adams, Harrison Bahr. Mr. Bahr is one of the founding members of the Cattleman."

"Mr. Bahr," Clint said, extending his hand.

Bahr took it tentatively, and asked, "Clint Adams . . . the Gunsmith?"

"That's right," Bags said, before Clint could respond.

"Are you here to help?" Bahr asked Clint.

"I'm just passing through, Mr. Bahr," Clint said. "I don't even know what you need help with."

"Well, I can tell you—"

"That won't be necessary, Mr. Bahr," Bags said. "Clint is just here as a friend. I'll be taking care of the matter we talked about."

"Well, all right," Bahr said, looking at Clint again. Then he pointed and added, "Just seems a shame not to use him while he's here."

Bahr turned and walked back to his table, where he quickly huddled with three other men he was sitting with and told them what he'd found out.

"And what's this matter you two were discussing?"

"You don't want to know."

"Seems a shame," Clint said, "not to tell me, since I'm here."

"All right," Bags said, "but remember, you asked for it."

THREE

Joe Bags took Clint to a corner table, where they both positioned themselves so that they could see the entire room.

"We're having a slight problem in town with a gang run by a guy named Ralph Markus."

"What's the slight problem?"

"Well . . . they kill people."

"I can see where that would bother some people."

"Well, they haven't killed anyone here in Abilene but they're in town, hanging around," Bags said.

"Why don't you ask them to leave?"

"That's easier said than done," Bags said. "There are half a dozen or more of them and just me and my deputy."

"So just talk to the leader."

"I'm going to," Bags said. "That's what I meant when I told Bahr I'd be takin' care of it."

"So then what's his problem?"

"He's also the head of the town council," Bags said, "and I've asked for more money to hire more deputies."

"And he refused?"

"Not yet," Bags said. "They're 'taking it under advisement.' You see my problem?"

"Yes," Clint said. "If you talk to Markus and get him and his men to leave, the council will say you don't need any more deputies. You handled it just fine with the one."

"Exactly."

"But you don't want to wait too long so that Markus and his gang really do start trouble—maybe even kill somebody."

"Exactly."

"Where have they killed?"

"Oklahoma, Missouri, to hear tell."

"To hear who tell?'

"Stories."

"Any paper out on them?"

"None that's crossed my desk."

"So you really can't just run them off."

"I could . . ." Bags said, letting it trail off.

"Uh oh . . ." Clint said.

". . . if you would help me."

"How did I see that coming?"

"Well, Bahr's right about one thing, Clint."

"And what's that?"

"It would be shame to let your presence here go completely to waste."

They finished their beers and left the Cattleman Club. Bags seemed oblivious to the stares they drew as they left. Clint wondered if his friend was really unaware of the way the club members looked at him, or if he just didn't care. Either way he thought it was dangerous and figured to say something about it before he left town—as soon as he figured out how to approach it.

"Okay," Clint said.

"Okay what?"

"I'll go with you to see Ralph Markus."

"I'm not looking for you to back any play I make," Bags hurriedly said. "Just a show of numbers."

"Three instead of two?" Clint asked. "Do you think that will make a difference?"

"When he finds out who you are, yes," Bags said. "You're not mad at me for this, are you?"

"Why should I be?" Clint said. "You didn't ask me to come here, and you're right about not using me while I'm here. If it'll make things easier for you, I'll be glad to help."

"That's great," Bags said. "You could also help me another way."

"How?"

"Talk to the kid."

"By the kid you mean your deputy?"

Bags nodded.

"I think Alex has the makings of a good deputy, Clint," Bags said. "He just needs somebody else to talk to besides me."

"I'll talk to him," Clint said.

"Thanks."

"If only to keep him from turning out the way you did."

When they entered the marshal's office McCord was right where he had been when Clint came in the first time.

"Why don't you go and get something to eat, Alex." Bags said. "Clint and I will hold down the fort here for a while."

"Okay," McCord said, standing up and reaching for his hat. "I'm really hungry."

"Just don't forget to come back," Bags said.

"Aw, come on," McCord said. "I only did that once."

"And once is enough."

"Where are you going to eat, Alex?" Clint asked. "Maybe I'll come by in a little while and have a slice of pie with you."

"Wow, that would be great!" McCord said. "There's a café on Front Street. The marshal knows where it is."

"I'll direct him," Bags said.

"Okay," McCord said excitedly. "Well then, I'll see you later."

"See you," Clint said, and watched the boy fly out the door with his feet off the ground.

"Thanks, Clint," Bags said.

"Sure," Clint said. "What else have I got to do?"

FOUR

"How long has the kid been your deputy?" Clint asked, after McCord had left the office.

"About a month."

"Why did you pick him?"

"Nobody else applied for the job."

"Is Abilene still as rough as it once was?"

"No," Bags said, "at least, it wasn't until Markus and his crew came to town."

"You mean they've affected the town so much that you can't get anyone to take the deputy's job?"

"Apparently, they have."

"So once they leave you'll be able to hire somebody else."

"I hope so."

"And keep Alex?"

"Oh yeah," Bags said. "I meant it when I said I thought he had the makings."

Clint frowned and said, "Maybe they're not readily evident."

"You're seein' him when he's all excited about meetin' you," Bags said. "He listens to orders—usually—and he doesn't back down."

"How do you know? Has he seen any action yet?"

"We have two prisoners in the back," Bags said. "He arrested both of them, alone."

"What for?"

Bags hesitated, then said, "That's not important."

"What did he arrest them for, Bags?"

The marshal hesitated again, then said, "Well, one was drunk and disorderly and the other one . . . shot a dog."

"Shot a dog?"

"That's right."

As Clint recalled Hickok used to get paid for every stray dog he shot.

"All right, so maybe they weren't major criminals, but he still didn't back down."

"That's fine, Joe," Clint said. "He's got to start somewhere."

"That's right."

"Good for him," Clint said.

They sat in silence for a few moments and then Clint asked, "Did he arrest them at the same time?'

"No," Bags said, "separately."

They sat silently for a few more moments and then Bags said, "Still pretty good, though."

"Fine," Clint said, "it's just fine." He stood up. "I think I'll go and have that pie."

When Clint arrived at the Front Street Café—clever name—he saw Alex McCord sitting at a table by the front window.

"What are you doing?" Clint asked.

McCord looked up at him and smiled.

"Whataya mean?"

"Why are you sitting at the window?"

"I want to be able to see the street, in case there's any trouble," McCord said. "I want to be ready."

"Kid," Clint said, "if you can see people in the street, they can see you."

"So?"

"So you make a perfect target sitting there."

McCord stared at Clint for a few moments, then his eyes widened and he said, "You mean . . . ?"

"Yes, I do," Clint said. "I mean you should change tables." Clint looked around. The place was fair-sized, and not crowded because it was actually between mealtimes.

"Let's take that table in the corner," Clint said. "You can see the whole room from there, and you can see out the front door."

"But I already ordered."

"They'll bring the food to a different table," Clint assured him. "Come on, move before somebody decides to take a shot at you."

McCord got up and followed Clint to the corner table. When he was with someone he liked or knew Clint usually took a corner table because it gave them each a wall to put their backs against.

When the waitress came out of the kitchen carrying McCord's food she saw that the table by the window was empty and she looked around curiously. When she spotted him she came walking over.

"Changed tables on me, huh?" she asked.

McCord didn't answer. He was staring at the girl and Clint knew that he didn't eat here for the food. She was about his age, very fresh-faced and pretty, with a slender body beneath a thin cotton dress. She had small breasts, but they were firm and reminded Clint of ripe peaches.

"That was my fault," Clint said. "I didn't want him to sit by the window with that shiny badge on his chest."

"Probably a good idea," she said, putting McCord's food down in front of him. "Who's your friend, Alex?"

"Uh," McCord said, roused from his stupor by the sound of her voice asking him a question. "Uh, this is Clint Adams. Clint, this is Mitzi."

"Pleased to meet you, Mitzi."

"Can I get you something to eat, Mr. Adams?" she asked.

"Just a piece of pie, Mitzi," he said. "Peach, if you have it, and some coffee."

"Peach pie and coffee," she said with a smile. "Comin' right up."

She went back to the kitchen and McCord watched her all the way.

"Pull your tongue in, kid, before somebody steps on it."

"Huh?" McCord looked at Clint. "Ain't she pretty?"

"Real pretty, kid," Clint said, "but how's the food here?"

"Food?" McCord repeated, and looked back at the kitchen door.

"Never mind," Clint said. "I'll find out for myself."

FIVE

Across town Ralph Markus sat in the Long Branch Saloon with two of his men, Carl Bankhead and Ruben Sierra. His three other men were undoubtedly elsewhere, indulging in their individual pleasures—whores, gambling, and playing horseshoes. It was Lonnie Fields who had a passion for horseshoes, but then they all knew he was touched.

"How much longer we got to wait?" Bankhead asked. "I thought we came here to take this bank."

"We did," Markus said, "but I kind of like it here."

"So what?" We ain't gon' rob the bank?" Sierra asked.

"Oh, we're gonna rob it," Markus said. "Don't worry about that."

"When?" Bankhead asked.

Markus gave him a hard look and said, "Don't worry about that, either, Carl."

"Look," Bankhead said, "we checked it out. This town's got one marshal and one deputy. Neither one of them can stop us, either alone or together. We got no worries with the law, Ralph."

"I know that."

"So what's the holdup?"

Markus made a pistol out of his forefinger and thumb, pointed it at Bankhead, and pulled the trigger. "That's funny."

"I wasn't tryin' to be funny."

"I know that, Carl," Markus said. "You don't have a sense of humor. That's what made it funny."

"I don't get it," Bankhead said.

Even Sierra laughed at that.

"Look, Carl," Markus said, leaning forward in his chair, "relax. That bank's gonna be empty by the end of the week."

Bankhead threw his hands in the air and said, "That's all I been tryin' to find out."

"You gotta relax," Markus said, sitting back, "or you'll never make it to my age."

"Whataya talkin' about?" Bankhead asked him. "We grew up together. We're the same damn age!"

Markus looked at Ruben Sierra, who laughed again, displaying an impressive set of gold teeth.

"Why don't you fellas go for a walk?' Markus asked. "I got some thinkin' to do before this place gets crowded."

"Yeah," Bankhead said, standing up. "I could use some air. You comin', amigo?"

"I will accompany you," Sierra said, also standing, "if only to keep you out of trouble."

"Me? Trouble? When do I ever get in trouble?"

He watched both men expectantly, and then said, "Why ain't you laughin'? That was a joke."

"Like I said, Carl," Markus replied, "you got no sense of humor."

As Bankhead and Sierra left the Long Branch, Markus went to the bar for another beer. He figured he had an hour before ranch hands and clerks got off work and started drifting in for a night's entertainment.

"Another one," he said to the bartender, "and make this one cold."

"They're all—uh, yes, sir. Cold one, comin' right up."

He hurried to get Markus the coldest beer he could. The outlaw accepted it without thanks, paid for it and took it with him to his table.

The Abilene bank had been on his list for a long time, but he hadn't gotten to where he was by being stupid. Abilene usually had some pretty tough and competent lawmen, dating all the way back to Bill Hickok and Bear River Tom Smith. Now, however, they had this fella Joe Bags, and finally Markus felt that the First Abilene Bank was ripe for the taking.

However, he'd been telling the truth when he told Bankhead that he liked Abilene. If he was going to settle down someplace in the near future he'd probably pick Abilene, or a town like it. It had a history, but it was still changing and growing. He liked that.

Of course, it was going to have to change and grow without any money in the bank, real soon.

Clint ate his pie real slow, watching the boy put his food away in between watching the girl walk back and forth, to and from the kitchen.

"Why don't you marry her?" Clint asked.

"Huh? Marry Mitzi? We ain't even never, ya know, done nothin'."

"Have you taken her to a dance? Or on a picnic? Anything like that?" Clint asked.

"Naw, nothin'."

"Why not?"

McCord shrugged sheepishly.

"You shy?"

"I guess I am."

"Want me to ask her for you?"

"Would ya?" asked the younger man, excited by the prospect.

"No, son," Clint said, "I'm afraid that's something you're going to have to do yourself."

SIX

Clint and McCord parted company out in front of the café. The deputy went back to work after profusely thanking Clint for keeping him company and getting him away from the window.

"How long are you gonna be in town, Clint?"

"Probably a few days, Alex."

"Then I'll see you again."

"Probably tomorrow."

"See you, then," McCord said, and hurried to get back to the marshal's office.

Clint shook his head as the young man almost ran off. He wasn't sure that Joe Bags was right about the kid having what it takes to be a deputy, but he was willing to give him the benefit of the doubt. Maybe after they talked once or twice more he'd calm down a bit.

He decided to go to a saloon and have a beer, spend some time just sitting and drinking. There were certainly not as many Hickok ghosts here as, say Deadwood, and he'd excised his Deadwood ghosts a long time ago. But he had not been in Deadwood when Hickok was killed, and he *was* here when there was trouble.

He chose the Long Branch simply because he was walking past it. He entered and found the place less than half full. There was plenty of room at the bar so he went there first and got himself a beer from a nervous-looking bartender. The man wasn't familiar to him, so he didn't think he was the reason for the case of nerves. It had to be somebody else in the place that was making the barkeep nervous.

Clint turned with his beer in hand and surveyed the place. Gaming tables were covered, as there were not enough people in the saloon yet to warrant starting the games. Most of the tables that were occupied had only one man at them, with several of them having two, but no more. Everyone seemed to be minding their own business, and he didn't see anyone who would be obvious as the bartender's source of nerves.

He turned back to the bar, leaned on it and worked steadily on his beer.

Alex McCord burst into the marshal's office and said, "I'm sorry I took so long, but I was talking to Clint—"

"Take it easy," Joe Bags said. "It's fine. Get your breath back."

McCord sat across from Bags and tried to get control of his breathing.

"Alex, you got to take it easy around Clint," Bags said. "You're gonna scare him out of town. After all, he's just a man."

"Just a man?" McCord repeated. "Jeez, Marshal, you've known him for years, you know he's a legend."

"He doesn't want to be a legend," Bags said. "He just

wants to be treated normal. You think you can do that for him?"

McCord frowned, not understanding why a man as famous as the Gunsmith would want to be treated like anyone else.

"Well . . . I guess I can."

"Good," Bags said. "A little less gushing and a lot more listening and you might learn something."

Bags stood up and put on his hat. "Come with me."

"Where we goin'?"

"We're gonna have a talk with Mr. Ralph Markus."

McCord stopped halfway out of his chair.

"Really?"

"Yes, really."

The deputy stood up the rest of the way, looking worried.

"What about the prisoners?"

"They're not going anywhere, Alex," Bags said. "They'll be here when we get back."

"How we gonna find him?"

"We'll just look, Alex," Bags said. "Are you not up to this?"

The young deputy hitched up his gunbelt, puffed out his chest and said, "Just show me where he is, Marshal."

Bags held out his hand and said, "Just take it easy, Alex. I'll do all the talking. You just have to stand there with me."

"I can do that, Marshal," McCord said. "I can stand there."

"Good," Bags said, "then let's go."

Clint finished his beer without incident. Nobody in the saloon seemed to recognize him, which suited him just fine.

He pushed his empty mug away, took one last look at the place and then walked out the batwing doors. Almost immediately he spotted Joe Bags and Alex McCord walking his way.

"What brings you two here?" Clint asked.

"We're lookin' for Ralph Markus," McCord said excitedly. Clint thought that this boy was going to have to calm down before he exploded. His eyes looked glassy and he seemed to be breathing real hard. "Is he in there?"

"Can't tell you that, Alex," Clint said, "because I don't know what the man looks like."

"We got word that Markus is in the Long Branch," Bags said. "Thought it was time I had that talk with him."

"That explains why the bartender is so nervous," Clint said.

"Want to tag along?" Bags asked.

Clint figured the question was for McCord's benefit, since he had already agreed to stand with Bags when he talked to the outlaw leader.

"Let's do it," he said.

SEVEN

They entered the saloon with Joe Bags in front, Clint and McCord flanking him. Once again Clint looked around, trying to guess who Ralph Markus was. He finally settled on a rough-looking character who was sitting alone, scowling into a half empty beer mug.

"There he is," Bags said. "Come on."

Clint was surprised when instead of approaching the hardcase with the half empty beer they walked up to a table where a young, pleasant-looking man sat, also alone. He didn't look much older than Deputy McCord.

"Markus?" Joe Bags said.

The young man looked up at Bags with completely guileless eyes. They were clear, blue and very innocent looking.

"Marshal," Markus said. "What can I do for you?"

"I thought it was time we had a talk."

"About what?"

"About you and your boys leavin' town."

Markus made a show of looking past the marshal at both Deputy McCord and Clint.

"Looks like one of your deputies forgot his badge, Marshal," the young outlaw said.

"He didn't forget," Bags said. "He's not a deputy. He's just a friend."

"Must be a good friend to back your play against me."

"I ain't makin' a play, Markus," Bags said. "I told you, I'm just here to talk."

"You're here to try and run me and the boys out of town, Marshal, and you only got two men helpin' you do it."

"Guess th-that depends on who the men are," McCord said, stammering slightly.

"Hey, the baby lawman speaks," Markus said.

"Ain't no younger than you," McCord said, belligerently.

Bags looked back at McCord and tried to silence him with a look.

"So who's your friend, Marshal?" Markus asked. He was wondering why this friend would make such a difference, that the marshal would pick this time to come and talk to him after he and his boys had been in town over a week, now.

Clint, on the other hand, was wondering why Bags, the bartender and probably most of the town were scared of this benign-looking young man. Did he really have such a reputation at such a young age?

"My friend's name is Clint Adams, Markus," Bag said. "He's just passin' through, but he agreed to help me out a little here. He's here for, um, moral support."

But Markus had stopped listening to Bags after he heard Clint's name. His benign eyes had suddenly become two chips of blue ice as they bored into Clint, who was now seeing what was under the surface of the innocent-looking face.

"The Gunsmith," Markus said.

"That's r-right!" McCord blustered.

Markus ignored him, as well, and kept his eyes on Clint.

"You had some high times in this town once, didn't you, Adams?" Markus asked.

"I've been here before."

"And now you're here again," the younger man said, "and I'm supposed to be scared?"

To the man's credit he did not look scared at all. He did, however, look interested.

"Maybe you're just supposed to be smart, Markus," Clint said.

"Get smart and pull me and my boys out of Abilene just because you're here?"

"That would be the smart thing to do," Bags said.

"You," Markus said, looking at Bags. "You couldn't even come and talk to me until your friend, here, came to town and agreed to stand with you. You and your deputy, you're nothin' to me."

"Now wait just a—"

"So I don't have to worry about you two," Markus went on, ignoring Joe Bags. "I just got to worry about one man, and since I got five men with me, all young and all good with a gun, I think I'll take my chances—especially against a legend as worn-out as the Gunsmith."

Markus took his eyes off all three men and looked away, unconcerned.

"Go on, get out, the three of you," he said. "Me and my boys ain't goin' nowhere."

"You're makin' a mistake, Markus," Bags said.

Markus looked at Bags, his expression cold.

"You made your mistake when you didn't brace us

the minute we got here, Marshal," he said. "We might have had second thoughts about stayin' if you'd shown any backbone at all. No, I don't think we've made a mistake at all. I think this town made the mistake when they made you their marshal."

Clint waited to see what Bags was going to do, and was disappointed when he simply turned and walked out. McCord looked confused, looked at Clint, then turned and followed Bags out.

"You still here?" Markus asked.

"If you hadn't made a mistake before, you made one now, Markus."

"And what's that?"

"You embarrassed that man," Clint said. "You put his back to the wall and gave him no choice. He'll have to stand up to you, now."

"With you by his side?"

"Maybe," Clint said. "I guess that's just something you'll have to wait to find out."

EIGHT

When Clint got outside both Bags and McCord were gone. They had probably gone back to the marshal's office, but Clint decided not to go looking for them. They were each probably embarrassed for their own reasons.

Clint was also embarrassed, but it was for his friend. He never would have thought that Joe Bags was cut out to be the marshal of a town like Abilene. A deputy, yes, or the sheriff of some smaller town, but not Abilene. Now it looked like he was right.

He knew Bags wouldn't want to see him right now, not after he'd allowed Ralph Markus to make him back down. As for Markus, Clint was sure that the young man's innocent looks were a major asset to him in his chosen profession as an outlaw. He, himself, had almost underestimated him at first sight, but he would not make that mistake again. He assumed that Markus's five men were also his age, which made them a gang of young, hungry lions. Put them in the middle of Abilene and you were just waiting for trouble.

Clint had to decide if he wanted to wait, or move on.

Inside the Long Branch Markus was sitting thinking about Clint Adams. Hearing his name had been a shock. A town that had been easy pickings had suddenly become a little harder, and he'd allowed it to happen. If he and his boys had taken the bank as soon as they arrived they'd have been long gone by the time the Gunsmith arrived in town. He knew he had put up a good front, but a man like Clint Adams was not to be taken lightly, not even at the age he was now. Why, Markus believed Adams was probably over forty!

He was going to have to gather his boys together tonight and come to a decision. It was time to hit the bank and get out.

He turned his head and saw the girls coming down the stairs. The covers were also coming off the gaming tables. He wasn't going to have to go looking for his men. They knew what time it was, and they'd be there any minute.

"That looks warm and flat," a girl's voice said.

He looked up and saw Dixie, a blonde with incredible breasts. They were big and round and solid and always looked as if they were going to come spilling out of her dress.

"I think it is," he said.

"Want a cold one?"

"That'd be great."

She picked up his mug, bending over to do so and giving him a nice, clear view down the front of her dress. They'd been eyeing each other for a few days, and tonight was going to have to be the night he got inside that dress. There was no way he was leaving Abilene without seeing Dixie naked.

No way.

When Clint got to his hotel he decided to sit outside rather than go in. He pulled a wooden chair over, leaned it against the front of the hotel and sat down. It was dusk, and would be dark soon. Bags would have to come out to make his rounds. By then maybe he would have collected himself and wouldn't be as embarrassed to see Clint.

Maybe.

In the marshal's office Bags was sitting at his desk, contemplating nothing. He was staring off into space. Across the desk from him sat McCord, who remained silent. They'd been sitting this way since the moment they came back from the saloon.

Finally, McCord spoke.

"I don't understand."

"What's to understand?" Bags asked. "I thought having Clint there with us would scare Markus into leaving. It didn't."

"So what do we do now?"

"I have to think about that."

After a few moments more of silence McCord said, "Marshal?"

"Yeah?"

"I was scared."

"Don't feel bad," Bags said. "So was I."

McCord didn't feel bad about being scared, but he did feel bad because Joe Bags had been scared. This was the man who was supposed to be his teacher, and he was afraid of an outlaw like Ralph Markus, who was no older than McCord himself. It was okay for McCord to be scared—he'd only been wearing a badge a short time. It shook him, though, that the man he looked up to was scared, and admitted it.

"Does that shock you?" Bags asked.

"I . . . well . . ."

"Don't let it," Bags said. "A man who can't admit he's scared is a fool, Alex. There's nothing wrong with being scared."

"Why are you so quiet, then?"

"I'm thinkin'."

"Marshal—"

"Alex," Bags said, "I can't think if you're gonna talk. Go and check on the prisoners."

"Yes, sir."

"In fact," Bags said, tossing the deputy the keys, "let them out. We got more important things to worry about."

NINE

It was almost dark, the streetlamps had all been lit and music was coming from the saloons by the time Joe Bags left his office and walked over to the hotel to find Clint sitting out front. Bags grabbed a chair, brought it over and sat down next to him.

"I didn't conduct myself very well, did I?" he asked.

"I'm not here to judge."

They sat in silence a few moments and then Clint said, "He didn't back down. That threw you off, didn't it? You thought I was going to be the big difference?"

"I guess I did." Bags pushed his hat back on his head and passed his hands over his eyes. "I should have known that his kind wouldn't back down."

"I didn't realize he'd be so young," Clint said. "He's too young to be smart, Joe."

"I figured that. I can't force them out of town, though."

"Not without shots being fired."

"I won't ask that of you."

"Thanks."

"It's my problem—mine and young Alex's."

"He'd get killed first thing," Clint said. "He's not ready for that."

Bags looked at Clint.

"I don't know that I am, either," he said. "Not to face six outlaws with Alex at my side."

"Joe—"

Bags held up his hands and stood up.

"I'm not askin', Clint," Bags said. "You can go or stay with no hard feelings from me. This is the kind of thing I signed on to take care of."

"There must be one or two others in town who'd stand with you, even if they won't wear a badge."

"You'd think," Bags said. "I'll see you tomorrow, I guess. Good night."

"Good night, Bags."

Clint watched his friend walk away and knew that when the time came to fire shots, he'd be right there with him. There was nothing else he'd be able to do.

Eventually, Markus ended up sitting in the Long Branch with Bankhead, Sierra and the other three—Lonnie Fields, Mike Paul and Ray Hogan.

"We're takin' the bank tomorrow mornin'," he said.

"Whoa," Hogan said. "Where'd that come from?"

"Why tomorrow?" Sierra asked.

"Why so soon?" Fields asked.

"Don't we have to check it out?" Paul asked.

"I've checked it out," Markus said. "It's not so soon. I've had this planned for days."

"So why are we going tomorrow?" Bankhead asked. "When we talked this afternoon—"

"I know what I said this afternoon," Markus said, "but things change."

"What's changed that much?" Sierra asked.

"I had a visit from the marshal today."

"So what?" Sierra asked.

"He's not a problem," Bankhead said.

"He had his deputy with him."

"He ain't no problem, either," Fields said. "He's just a kid."

"He's our age," Hogan said.

"Maybe so," Fields said, "but he ain't like us."

"What's changed, Ralph?" Sierra asked again.

"He had another man with him," Markus said. "Clint Adams."

He waited for that to sink in.

"Clint Adams?" Fields asked.

"The Gunsmith?" Hogan said.

"That's right."

"Is Adams a deputy?" Sierra asked.

"No," Markus said, "worse. He's a friend of the marshal's."

"So he'll back his play?" Bankhead asked.

"That's right."

They all sat quietly for a while, and then Mike Paul asked, "So why don't we just leave town?"

"Give up the bank?" Fields asked.

"Because of one man?' Bankhead added. "I don't think so."

"That one man is the Gunsmith," Paul said. "I ain't lookin' forward to facing no Gunsmith."

"We're not gonna," Markus said. "That's why we're gonna hit the bank in the morning, when they first open, before they're ready for us."

"What makes you think they won't be ready tomorrow?" Fields asked.

"It's too soon," Markus said. "They just braced me

today. They won't expect us to move so fast."

They were all quiet again, and then Sierra said, "It sounds good to me."

"What about the rest of you?" Markus asked.

In turn they all nodded until Bankhead said, "Okay, Ralph, we're all in."

"Good," Markus said, pulling his chair closer, "then this is how it's gonna go . . ."

TEN

The next morning, fifteen minutes before the bank was due to open, Ralph Markus was across the street, standing in a doorway. In doorways to his right and left were Ruben Sierra and Carl Bankhead. Down the street with six saddled horses was Lonnie Fields. Behind the bank were both Ray Hogan and Mike Paul.

They were all in position.

Twelve minutes before the bank was due to open Marshal Joe Bags was in his room over the general store getting dressed. He was wondering what to have for breakfast, where to have it and what he was going to do about Ralph Markus and his gang.

Ten minutes before the bank was due to open Clint Adams was rolling over in bed, wondering if he should get up and have breakfast or stay where he was for another half an hour. He was also wondering why he didn't have a woman there next to him.

• • •

Five minutes before the bank was due to open Deputy Alex McCord stuck his hand in his pocket and came out with his pay for the past two weeks. He hadn't been able to get to the bank yet, but he'd gotten up early this morning so he could get over there when it opened and make a deposit into his savings account. He already had nearly fifty dollars in there!

Two minutes before the bank was due to open the bank manager, Gerald Hawkins, came out of his office and looked at the clock on the wall, comparing it to his pocket watch. In the teller's cages were the two tellers, Sam Daltry and young Mary Evans, the new, pretty teller he'd hired just last week to replace Mrs. Wintergreen, who had retired. He'd hired Mary because she appeared to be smart, trainable and was so pretty he could hardly bear it. It gave him a new reason to come to work every morning, especially after sitting across the table from his wife at breakfast—or, at least, the old woman his wife had gotten to be.

With one minute to go he started for the front door.

With thirty seconds to go Markus stepped from his doorway and started across the street. Sierra and Bankhead stepped out their respective doorways and followed.

Behind the bank Paul said to Hogan, "Get ready."

"I been ready," Hogan said nervously. He hated the waiting. The actual robbing was fine, but the waiting got on his nerves and made his hands sweat.

With twenty second left Lonnie Fields watch as the deputy walked past him, ignoring him and the six horses, heading toward the bank.

"Shit!" he said.

• • •

As Ralph Markus was walking across the street he wasn't thinking about the bank robbery. He was thinking about the night he'd had with Dixie. Damn, but those breasts were the biggest, firmest he'd ever sunk his teeth into. She had the cutest face he'd ever seen, almost like a little girl, sometimes, but her body was all woman. Too bad he hadn't gotten to her sooner, and had only had one night with her, but who knew Clint Adams was going to come to town and ruin even that for him. He was thinking that maybe it wasn't such a good idea to hit the bank and head out of town. Maybe he should take care of Adams first.

No, the others wouldn't go for that at all. They all wanted to grab the money and run, and being the good leader he was, that's what they were going to do.

As Gerald Hawkins unlocked the front door Ralph Markus pushed it open and stepped inside.

"Good morning, sir," Hawkins said. "How can we—"

Markus stuck a gun in Hawkins's face and said, "Let's just cooperate and nobody will get hurt."

"Dear me," Hawkins said, and fainted.

ELEVEN

"Drag him somewhere!" Markus said as Bankhead and Sierra came in behind him. He was talking to Bankhead. To Sierra he said, "Open the back door and let the others in!"

"Right."

Markus pointed his gun at the two tellers, a plain-looking young man and a very pretty young woman. She didn't have Dixie's breasts, but she did have a prettier face. Too bad he didn't have time . . .

"Put all the money in a bag, now!" hc said to them.

"Yessir," the man said, and hurried to obey.

"You can't do this," Mary Evans said.

"Mary," Sam Daltry said, "don't—"

"No," she said, angrily, "they can't get away with this. What have you done to poor Mister Hawkins?"

"I didn't do nothin' to him, lady," Markus said. "He fainted dead away, like a girl."

"We got to wake him up," Bankhead said. "He's the only one who can open the safe."

"Wake him up, then," Markus said. He looked at Mary. "Does anyone else work here?"

"Yes," she said, "and they'll be here soon."

"That's all right," Markus said, "we'll be gone soon. We—"

He spun around as the front door opened. If the bank manager hadn't fainted Bankhead would have been watching the door. It opened and the deputy walked in. When he saw Markus with his gun out he got a dumb look on his face and froze.

"Take it easy, Deputy," Markus said. "Carl, get his gun before he does somethin' stupid."

Before McCord could move Bankhead had disarmed him.

"Get him over by the manager and keep trying to wake him up," Markus said.

"W-what are you doin?" McCord demanded.

"They're robbing the bank, Alex," Mary Evans said. "You're the law. Do something!"

Markus gave her a look and asked, "What would you suggest he do, ma'am? He ain't even armed."

"Well," she said, hardly mollified by that revelation, "he's the law, he should do something!"

Markus looked at McCord, shook his head and said, "What a stupid woman, eh?"

But McCord didn't think Mary Evans was so stupid. He was the law and he should be doing something.

But what?

Joe Bags pulled on his boots and decided on flapjacks for breakfast. That would fill him up for the day and keep him going until supper. He rarely had more than a beer for lunch.

As he left his rooms he decided to walk to the hotel

and see if Clint wanted to have some flapjacks with him. He was still stinging over the scene at the saloon the day before with Ralph Markus, but he knew Clint was his friend and would not judge him harshly for that.

That's what friends were for.

Clint rolled out of bed, his stomach rumbling and complaining. Breakfast was the first order of the day, and the hotel dining room was as good a place as any—especially since the only other place he really knew of to eat was the café where he'd had the pie with Alex McCord, and the pie had not been very good.

But then the deputy hadn't gone there for the food, had he? Clint didn't think Alex McCord should even be a deputy. That boy's biggest problem should have been how to get that pretty waitress to go on a picnic with him. He did not even think that being a lawman was in the boy's future.

He would remember that thought later.

Gerald Hawkins came to and sat up.

"What happened?" he asked.

"You fainted like a damn girl," Markus said, "and you're throwin' off my timetable. Carl, get him to his feet."

Bankhead hauled the manager to his feet while the man was still trying to figure out what had happened. When he looked at Markus and saw the gun he remembered, and his eyes started to roll back into his head.

"Whoa, hold on there, bank manager," Markus shouted, "don't go out on us again!"

The shouting snapped Hawkins to and he looked around. When he saw McCord and his badge his eyes widened.

"Deputy," he said, anxiously, "you've got to do something."

"It's amazing," Ralph Markus said to Alex McCord, "how many of these people want you to go and get yourself killed, ain't it?"

TWELVE

Joe Bags entered the hotel lobby just as Clint was coming down the stairs.

"I was thinkin' about flapjacks," Bags said.

"Sounds good to me," Clint said. "Here?"

"Why not?"

They went into the dining room together.

"Open the safe," Ralph Markus said to Hawkins.

"I told you I can't," Hawkins said. "It's on a time lock."

"What's that?"

"It's something new," the bank manager said. "I can't open the safe until nine-thirty."

Markus looked at the clock on the wall. It was only ten after nine. They couldn't stay around another twenty minutes. In fact, in five minutes Lonnie Fields was going to bring six horses to the front of the bank. There was no way that was going to go unnoticed.

By this time both Hogan and Mike Paul were in the bank.

"Get behind those teller windows and find all the cash you can," Markus told them.

"You believe him?" Bankhead asked. "That he can't open the safe? That stuff about a time lock?"

"Look at him!" Markus said. "He's about to faint again. You think he has the nerve to lie to us?" He looked over at Paul and Hogan. "What's going on?"

"They put all the money they had in these bags, Ralph," Paul said, holding up two bank bags, one in each hand. He shook them. "Feels like we didn't do too bad."

"All right," Markus said. "Carl, is Lonnie out front with the horses yet?"

Bankhead looked out the window.

"Not yet—wait, here he comes."

"Okay," Markus said, 'we got to get out of here before another customer comes in, like the deputy here."

"Wait a minute," Sierra said. "What you doin' here, Deputy?"

McCord didn't answer. Sierra smacked him in the back of the head, knocking his hat off.

"Come on, Deputy," Markus said. "Don't play hero. Answer the man's question."

Grudgingly, McCord said, "I come to make a deposit."

"A deposit," Sierra said. "That means he got money on him."

"Hand it over, Deputy," Markus said.

McCord looked appalled.

"No! It's my pay."

"A week's pay?" Markus asked.

"Two weeks' pay," McCord said, before he could stop himself.

"Well," Markus said, "we sure can't leave two weeks of a deputy's pay behind, can we, boys?"

"You can't—"

"Shut up," Sierra said, and this time when he slapped McCord behind the head it was with his gun. The deputy went down to one knee and Sierra went through his pockets and came out with his money.

"Lookee here," he said, holding the money aloft triumphantly. "Two weeks' pay for the deputy!"

"Give it back!" McCord snapped, and reached for it. Sierra took one step back, drew his gun and fired a round into McCord's chest. The deputy's mouth snapped open in shock, and then he fell onto his back.

"Stupid!" Markus said. "Let's get out of here!"

Bankhead opened the door. As planned he and Sierra went out the door first. Then Hogan and Paul, with Mike Paul still carrying the two money bags.

"You folks just stay where you are for a while and nobody else is gonna get hurt.

"You . . . you shot him in cold blood," Mary Evans said.

"Well, ma'am," Markus said, "you wanted him to try to do something and he did. What did you expect would happen?"

"I . . . I don't . . . you killed him!"

It got very quiet then and they could all hear the gurgling sounds coming from Alex McCord. He was lying on his back and his lungs were filling up with blood. As he tried to breathe he was, instead, drowning.

"Well," Markus said, "not yet."

He stepped to McCord so that he was standing over him. The deputy's eyes were open and glassy, but he could still see Markus point the gun at his face. His eyes widened and then the gun went off, and Alex McCord's world went black.

Markus looked at Mary Evans and said, "Now I killed him."

At the sound of the first shot both Clint and Bags looked at each other.

"What could that be?" Clint asked.

"Almost anything," Bags said around a mouthful of flapjacks.

"How often does that happen?'

"Once in a while," Bags said. "Somebody blowin' off steam. As long as there's not a second shot I think we're o—"

He was cut off by a second shot, and they were both on their feet and out the door.

THIRTEEN

They could hear horses, like receding thunder, as they ran in the direction of the bank. As they came out the front door men were running past them. It was clear that Bags had guessed right about the shots coming from the bank. They took off along with a dozen other men, but by the time they reached the bank the robbers were gone, the dust from their horses still swirling.

"I'll need a posse!" Bags shouted to the men.

They all looked at each other, and then at the marshal, but nobody volunteered, and nobody moved.

"Well then why did you come running over here if you weren't gonna do something?" Bags demanded.

"Curiosity," Clint said. "It controls men's feet."

They hurried toward the bank and ran inside. There were three people there, standing and staring down at a fourth.

"Jesus," Bags said. "Alex."

Clint and Bags ran to Alex, but it was obvious that he was dead.

"They just shot him," Mary Evans said. "He wasn't even standing up, and they shot him."

"What happened?" Bags demanded.

"They wanted his money," Mary said, "the money he'd brought to deposit. Two weeks' pay, he said. They knocked him down and took the money, then one of them shot him in the chest when he tried to get it back. But he was still alive, so before they left another one, the leader, shot him in the face while he was lying on his back."

"Which one?" Clint asked.

"Was it Markus?" Bags demanded. "Ralph Markus? Was it the Markus gang?"

"Yes," she said, "yes, they called him Ralph."

"Damn it!" Bags said. He was still on one knee by McCord, and he looked down at his dead deputy. "Stupid, stupid kid."

"Marshal," the bank manager, Hawkins, said, "you've got to go after them. They got the bank's money."

"The bank's money?" Clint asked. "I thought it was the depositor's money."

"It's the same thing," Hawkins said.

"Did they get into the safe?" Clint asked.

"No," Hawkins said, "the safe is on one of those new time locks."

"They got the money from the tellers' cages," Mary Evans said. "All of it."

"We've got to get after them," Bags said, standing up.

"Not now, Bags."

"Before they get too far!"

"The two of us?" Clint asked. "On what horses? You just going to go out into the street and grab somebody's horse? We need time to get saddled and outfitted. We're going to have to track them, not chase them. We need a posse."

"You saw those men out there," Bags said. "They won't ride with a posse."

"Somebody in this town will," Clint said.

"I-I will," Sam Daltry said.

Clint looked at the teller. He was a slightly built man no older than Alex McCord. And Clint had the feeling he was volunteering only to impress the other teller, the pretty girl.

"All right," Clint said, "you're in the posse."

"What?"

"You volunteered, didn't you?"

Daltry wet his lips. He couldn't back out now, not in front of Mary. "Well . . . yes."

"See?" Clint said. "Now there's three of us."

"I don't have a gun!" Daltry snapped, as if he'd just thought of it.

Clint leaned down, undid McCord's gunbelt and pulled it free. Then he turned and tossed it to the teller, who caught it awkwardly.

"Now you've got a gun. Got a horse?"

"Yes, sir."

"Fine." Clint looked at Bags. "Take two hours to put together a posse and get outfitted. By then the gang will have committed themselves to a direction. We'll track them."

"I can't—I'm not a good tracker."

"There must be someone in town who can track," Clint said. "If not, I'll do it."

"We can get going sooner than two hours," Bags said.

Clint grabbed Bags by the arm and pulled him over to one side.

"You've got to get yourself together," Clint said, in almost a whisper.

"Look what they did to him!"

"They killed him," Clint said. "Nothing's going to change that. We've got to get the body over to the undertaker, and put together as much of a posse as we can. Two hours, Bags. No sooner. They're not going to get away. I guarantee it."

"You'll stick with it until we catch them?"

"I will," Clint said. "You're going to have to decide if you will."

"What do you mean?"

"You can only go so far and then you'll be out of your jurisdiction," Clint said. "Your badge won't mean anything. You've got to decide how far you're going to go."

"I'm going all the way," Bags said. "If not for me Alex would still be alive. If I had forced them out of town sooner—"

"That's another thing," Clint said, flicking Bags's badge with a fingernail. "While you're wearing this badge this isn't personal. Get ahold of yourself and stay controlled. Be a lawman, Bags."

Bags stared at Clint for a few seconds and Clint could see the younger man getting hold of himself.

"All right," the marshal finally said, "all right, two hours, and then we go."

FOURTEEN

In two hours they got more volunteers than Bags had expected. Clint, however, thought it was a direct result of the fact that the bank clerk, Sam Daltry, had been the first. A lot of the men were afraid to refuse once they realized that the mild-mannered clerk was included.

"I don't care why they volunteered," Bags said, in his office, "only that they did. We're leavin' in fifteen minutes."

"Right," Clint said. He didn't share his other thoughts about the posse with Bags, either. He had seen one man in the batch—and there were a dozen—who would stick with them when the going got rough.

Bags went to the gun rack and removed a Greener shotgun with side-by-side barrels.

"You want one?" he asked Clint, before he locked the rack up.

"I'll stick with my own guns, thanks."

As Bags was locking the rack up the door opened and a man stepped in. He was a bored-looking man, average height and weight with nothing to recommend him or differentiate him from any of the other posse men except for the fact that he *did* look bored. In fact, if he was as bored as he looked Clint thought he might soon be asleep.

The man fixed his drowsy eyes on them and said, "I hear you're looking for posse men."

"That's right," Bags said. "Do you have any experience?"

"More than the men I see gathering outside," the man replied. "Storekeepers, the lot of them."

"Most of them, yes," Bags said. "It's their money that was taken out of the bank, after all."

"That bunch," the man said, "will turn back at the first sign of trouble. Every one of them."

"And you won't?" Clint asked, wishing the man hadn't spoken the very words he himself had been thinking only moments before.

"No," the man said, "I would sign on for the long haul."

"Any special talents?" Bags asked.

"I can track."

Bags looked at Clint, who shrugged.

"Got a gun?" Bags asked.

"No."

Bags unlocked the gun rack and said, "Take one. How about a horse?"

"I got a horse," the man said, "and I don't got a gun because I don't need one."

"How do you defend yourself, then?" Bags asked.

Suddenly, without warning, a knife was quivering in the wooden bar that was used to lock the gun rack. Neither Bags nor Clint had seen the man throw it.

"You're hired," Bags said.

"Money?" the man asked.

"Three dollars a day," Bags said. "Only because you have no other stake in this."

The man walked to where his knife was still quivering and retrieved it. It was a big Bowie which had somehow been modified for throwing.

"Badge?" the man asked.

"You want one?" Bags asked.

"Don't need it," the man said. "Just thought you might need a deputy."

"No," Bags said, "I don't want any more deputies."

"Fine with me."

"What's your name?" Clint asked.

"Damien."

"Damien what?"

"Just Damien."

"Well, just Damien," Clint said, sticking out his hand, "I'm Clint Adams, this is Marshal Joe Bags. Welcome aboard."

"I know who you are," Damien said, shaking Clint's hand, and then the marshal's. "It'll be an honor to ride with you, Mr. Adams."

"Just call me Clint."

"All right, Clint."

Bags was gathering up his saddlebags and shotgun and started for the door, saying, "Let's go."

As Damien and Clint followed Clint asked, "Can you track as good as you can throw a knife?"

"Better," Damien said, without inflection or expression.

"That I've got to see."

Outside the rest of the men were mounting up, or already mounted and waiting for Bags and Clint.

Clint had already brought Eclipse over from the livery. Damien's horse was out in front of the marshal's office, as was Bags's.

Bags mounted up and addressed the men.

"You men have all lost money," he said. "I realize that. But I lost a deputy. What I say goes from now until we catch the bastards who killed him. Is that understood?"

Most of the men nodded and said yes, but one man pointed at Damien and asked, "Who's he?"

"His name is Damien," Bags said. "He's our tracker."

"We gonna need a tracker to follow six outlaws on horseback?" another man asked.

"If the trail goes cold," Bags said, "we're gonna need a tracker."

Somewhat mollified the two questioning men fell silent but still eyed Damien with suspicion, as he was a stranger.

"All right then," Bags said, "let's go and get the sons-of-bitches!"

FIFTEEN

Ralph Markus and his gang rode for several hours before he gave them a chance to rest their horses. All except Lonnie Fields.

"Lonnie, ride back a ways and see if they're after us," he ordered.

"Aw, Ralph," Fields said, "I'm tired like everybody else—"

"You let that deputy get by you," Markus said. "If it wasn't for you I wouldn't have had to kill him."

"Oh, awright . . ."

"I thought I killed the deputy," Sierra said as Lonnie rode away.

"You put him down," Markus said, "but you didn't kill him. I did that."

"So that's what the second shot was," Sierra said. "I thought maybe you put a bullet into that bank manager. I'm still not convinced that he was telling us the truth about that safe."

"Maybe he wasn't," Markus said, "but we didn't have the time to stick around and find out for sure, did we?"

"I suppose not."

Bankhead came over and said, "How about we count up the take?"

"Not yet," Markus said.

"Why not?"

"Because we're not camping, we're just resting the horses," Markus said. "When we stop for the night we'll count it up and split it up."

"Ralph—"

"That's the way we always do it, Carl."

"Yeah, okay."

Markus raised his voice. "All of you see to your horses. Make sure they're fit. Anybody goes lame they're gonna get left behind."

"With their cut," Hogan said.

"That's right," Markus said. "With their cut."

As the men saw to their horses Markus thought about the other reason he didn't want to count the take just yet. There wasn't going to be nearly as much money involved as he had originally told everyone there would be. He didn't want anybody getting mad enough to try to go back to town to get the rest. He didn't need anyone doing anything stupid right now. He was already disappointed in both Lonnie Fields and Ruben Sierra because of what happened with the deputy. They could have gotten away without firing a shot if that deputy hadn't walked in. And with a dead deputy that marshal was less likely to give up looking for them that easily.

Not to mention Clint Adams.

Markus waited for Lonnie to come back and tell him if they were being followed.

As everyone knew would be the case, they didn't need a tracker in the beginning. The trail was only two hours old and easy to follow. After about an hour Damien rode up next to Clint.

"They haven't split up yet."

"No," Clint said, "I noticed that."

"Be harder to trail them if they did," the other man said. "They must know that."

Clint looked at Damien. He realized the look on his face was more hangdog than boredom, as if he was always disappointed in something. In the office he'd put the man in his thirties but now he elevated that estimate and made him early forties. Certainly old enough to be disappointed in life.

"Thcy probably haven't divided the take, yet," Clint said. "These are young men. They won't go anywhere without their cut."

"You got that right, if they're as young as you say," Damien said. Seemingly satisfied with Clint's explanation the man fell silent and drifted away from Clint's side, only to be replaced by Joe Bags.

"What'd Damien want?"

Clint explained the tracker's concerns.

"That was good thinkin', though," Bags said. "More than we're gonna get out of the rest of these men."

Clint looked around at the other posse men and realized how right Bags was. He also knew that he and Damien were right about them. They were already beginning to look uncomfortable. A few more hours and most of them would be ready to turn back. When you're bone tired and you realize you might be riding into gunplay, all of a sudden money doesn't seem so important. Their initial anger at having their money stolen from the bank would wear off soon enough.

"You figure any of these men to stick?" Clint asked Bags.

"I been thinkin' about it since Damien said what he said," Bags answered, "and what you were thinkin'."

"And?"

"One or two, maybe," Bags said.

"That'd make five of us," Clint said. "Enough, I guess."

"And what happens when they do split up?" Bags asked.

"I think we're going to have to worry about that when the time comes, Joe," Clint said. "We've got enough to worry about right now. Why look for more? Maybe they won't split up."

"Yeah," Joe Bags said, doubtfully, "maybe they won't—but I sure ain't gonna count on that."

SIXTEEN

When Lonnie Fields returned and told Ralph Markus that he didn't see anyone on their trail Markus decided they'd camp for the night—soon.

"Just because they're not on our tails now doesn't mean they won't be coming," he told the others.

"What are they waiting for?" Hogan asked.

"They're putting a posse together," Markus said. "It's Adams. He's keeping that marshal from going off half-cocked after the death of his deputy."

"He's gonna care more about that than the money," Bankhead said.

"That's for sure," Markus agreed. "We'll camp tonight, split the money and then separate."

"Ray and I can ride—" Mike Paul started to say, but Markus cut him off midsentence.

"Nobody stays together," he said. "We go in six different directions. Anybody wants to meet up later can do it. We want to give them as many trails to follow as we can, just in case they don't have enough men."

"Sounds good to me," Sierra said. "I don't care if I

ever see any of you sons-of-bitches again." He was smiling when he said this, to take the sting away, just in case someone didn't know he was kidding.

"It's a sound plan, Ralph," Bankhead said. "Anybody here disagree?"

They all shook their heads that they didn't disagree, or nodded their heads that they agreed. Either way, the plan was set.

"Okay then," Markus said, "let's mount up. We still got a few good hours before we camp."

"Think they'll camp for the night?" Bags asked Clint during a short stop to rest the horses—and the storekeepers who weren't used to being on horseback.

"Oh, they'll camp," Clint said.

"How do you know?" Bags asked.

"Because Markus will realize that we're tracking him, and not following him," Clint said. "He's going to want to camp and split the money, and then probably separate."

"Three in one direction, two in another, like that?"

"I guess we'll have to wait and see," Clint said. "They might just decide to all go their separate ways."

Bags looked stricken.

"If they do that how do we track them?" he asked. "How do we catch the man who killed Alex?"

"We track them one at a time," Clint said. "It's that simple. Eventually we'll catch up to the man who pulled the trigger."

"Markus."

"Another man shot him first, according to the girl's story," Clint reminded him.

"Yeah, but Markus finished him," Bags said. "Shot

him like a dog while he was lying on his back on the floor."

"Take is easy, Bags."

"Don't worry," Bags said, "I'm in control."

He went off to address the rest of the posse. Clint wasn't at all sure his friend really was under control at all.

When the gang camped for the night they were impatient to split up the money.

"Get the bags," Markus said to Bankhead. "We might as well get this over with."

They sat around the fire and watched as Markus opened each bag and dumped out the contents.

"That doesn't look bad for not being able to get into the safe," Bankhead said.

"It looks pretty damn good," Markus said. "I wonder—" He stopped and snapped his fingers.

"What?" Sierra asked.

"Payday," Markus said. "That's why they had so much money in the tellers' cages. Today was payday."

"Don't people get paid in cash?" Lonnie Fields asked. He was asking because he'd never had an honest job in his life.

"Some folks get paid with a piece of paper," Markus said, "a chit or voucher or something, that they have to take to the bank and redeem for money. That must be the case in most of the businesses in Abilene."

They all sat there for a while and looked at the pile of money, illuminated only by the light of the campfire.

"Are you gonna count it?' Hogan asked, anxiously.

"Yeah, I'm gonna count it," Markus said. "Meanwhile, somebody start some coffee."

"You really wanna do that?' Bankhead asked. "Somebody could smell it and—"

"They won't reach this point until some time tomorrow," Markus assured him. "By that time we'll be split up. Meanwhile, I need some coffee tonight."

"Anybody think to bring some food?' Mike Paul asked.

They all looked rather chagrined and Bankhead said, "Well, this was put together real quick."

"I got some beans in my saddlebags," Paul said, and beamed.

"Well, get 'em!" Lonnie Fields said. "I'm starved."

Markus looked at Bankhead and said, "See? Mike ain't as dumb as you say he looks."

"Hey!" Mike Paul said.

SEVENTEEN

Damien sat alone while he ate. Bags and Clint sat together, and the townsmen formed their own group.

"What do you think of him?" Bags asked, indicating Damien, who was sitting across the camp. While he ate his head seemed cocked, as if he was listening intently.

"I like him," Clint said.

"Why?"

"He's quiet," Clint said, around a mouthful of beans. He was glad he'd made Bags wait two hours before pursuing the robbers. He'd been on hastily put together posses before, and it usually meant going hungry for most of the hunt. "No complaints, unlike that group."

They looked over at the townsmen, who between mouthfuls seemed to be discussing a variety of ailments brought on by a day in the saddle.

"They're not gonna last much longer," Bags said. He put his plate of beans on the ground between his feet, not quite finished with it. He picked up his coffee and slurped it. "Are we gonna catch 'em, Clint?"

"We will," Clint said. "What we do with them when we catch them will depend."

"On what?"

"On how many of us there are."

"Count on three, I guess," Bags said. "You, me and Damien."

"So you like him, too?"

"I think he'll stick," Bags said. "Can't say yet that I like him."

Bags put his coffee down, picked up his beans and finished them.

"More coffee?" he asked Clint. "I'm getting some."

"Sure."

The closest group to the fire were the townsmen. When Bags went among them to get to the coffeepot they spoke to him briefly. He responded shortly, then walked back to Clint and handed him his fresh cup of coffee.

"What'd they want?" Clint asked.

"They wanted to know how much longer I'd be needin' them."

"What did you say?"

"I told them not much longer if they continued bitchin' and moanin' all the time."

Clint finished his beans and put the plate down between his feet.

"It's my fault, you know," Bags said.

"What is?"

"Alex getting killed."

"How do you figure?' Clint asked. "You didn't put him in that bank."

"I put the badge on him," Bags said. "I tried to make a lawman out of him when he probably wasn't fit for it."

"I'll repeat," Clint said, "you didn't put him in that bank, and he would have been there, badge or not."

"He was there to put his pay in the bank."

"No matter what job he had he would have been putting his pay in the bank," Clint said.

"But if he didn't think of himself as a lawman he wouldn't have tried anything."

"He tried something because they were taking his money," Clint said. "Look, you can make yourself crazy with that kind of thinking. He got killed and it's a real sad thing, but it wasn't your fault any more than it was mine."

"Yours? Why would it be yours?"

"He idolized me, didn't he?" Clint asked. "Wanted to be like me? Isn't that what you said? Maybe he was doing what he thought I would do."

"That's crazy!" Bags said. "You didn't have anything to do with him getting killed."

"Well," Clint said, "that's how much sense your reasoning makes to me, too."

Bags hesitated, then said, "Ah, maybe you're right. Look, I don't want to put any of them on watch tonight." He was changing the subject and indicating the townsmen again. "How about you, me and Damien split it?"

"Fine with me."

"I'll get them to turn in."

"And I'll go and tell Damien."

They stood up went their separate ways, Bags taking his and Clint's plate along with him. Clint took his coffee over to where Damien was sitting. The dour-faced man had finished his beans and was drinking his coffee.

"You, me and the marshal will split the watch, Damien."

"Figured as much," the man said, without looking at

Clint. "That bunch ain't good for nothin' but bitchin' and whinin'."

"Our thoughts exactly."

"Won't last tomorrow."

"Probably not."

Now Damien looked at him.

"What we gonna do if they all turn back?"

"The marshal and I will go on," Clint said. "What you do will be up to you."

"I'll go on," Damien said. "Signed up for the long haul."

"Good," Clint said. "I figured we could count on you."

"I'll take the first watch, if you don't mind," Damien said. "Got my ears open, anyway."

"Fine," Clint said. "I'll relieve you."

Damien nodded.

"You want a rifle to stand watch with?"

"Don't need it."

"Just to fire a warning shot if anything happens."

Damien seemed to think that over a moment, then said, "If you think it's necessary."

"I do," Clint said. "I'll loan you mine."

"Much obliged."

"More coffee?"

"I'll just finish this."

"I'll make sure there's a pot on for you if you need it during the night," Clint said.

"Again, obliged."

"No," Clint said, "I think the marshal and I are obliged to you, Damien."

"For what?'

"For making sure that he and I aren't alone out here."

"Just didn't have nothin' else to do in town, is all," Damien said, with a shrug.

"You mind me asking what you were doing in Abilene in the first place?"

Clint asked.

"Passin' through," he said. "You?"

"I was just there visiting some ghosts."

Damien looked at him.

"What?"

Clint smiled and said, "I'll explain it to you some time."

EIGHTEEN

"Twenty-seven thousand split six ways," Ralph Markus said, after he'd finished counting the money. It was actually twenty-seven thousand three hundred and eighty-four, but he decided to round it out. He'd just keep the odd three hundred and eighty-four dollars himself for planning the robbery.

"How much is that each?" Lonnie Fields asked.

"Four thousand five hundred," Markus said.

"Jeez!"

It was a lot of money to all of them. Markus, however, had been imagining how much they would have gotten if they'd been able to get the safe open.

The count had taken place several hours ago, however, and now Markus was sitting awake and on watch while the others slept. He was trying to decide his future. Once they all split up did he want to get back together with any of them again? He knew one person he would like to have gotten together with again, and that was the saloon girl, Dixie. He wondered what she would do if he sent her train fare or stage fare to meet him someplace.

He thought back to that last—and only—night they had together . . .

Dixie had taken him to her room as soon as she was finished working, seemingly as anxious to be with him as he was to be with her.

"I been wonderin' how long it would take you to get around to this," she said, as she closed the door behind him.

"I guess I'm a little slow."

"Not slow," she said, approaching him, "just young."

This close she looked great, he thought. So what if she was a little older than he was. He kissed her then, tentatively at first, but then she melted against him and leaned into the kiss and it went on, open-mouthed, for quite a long time. As heady as the kiss was, though, he was still very aware of her very large breasts pressing into his chest. He wanted to see them.

As if reading his mind she broke the kiss and stepped back. She slid the straps of the dress from her shoulders and pulled the dress down so that her breasts were bare. They were the largest he'd ever seen, with heavy, round undersides and dark nipples that were already distended. His mouth went dry as she dropped the dress to the ground and stepped out of it. She'd been wearing no undergarments and was now totally and gloriously naked.

Her hips were wide, her thighs rounded, as she did a slow turn for him he saw that her butt was solid. It was her breasts, however, that completely held his fascination.

"You want to touch them, don't you?" she asked.

He nodded, unable to form the word.

"What is it about you men and my chest?"

He wet his lips and said, "You're beautiful."

"And you're sweet," she said. "All right, then, what are you waiting for?"

He reached for her but she stepped back and said, "Oh no. First you got to get naked, too."

"But—"

She slid her hands beneath her breasts and cupped them, then rubbed them with her palms. The sight of her rubbing her own nipples, biting her lips and moaning, was almost too much for him to bear.

"You want me, don't you?"

"Yes."

"You want these, don't you?" She used the thumb and forefinger of each hand to pinch her nipples.

"Y-yes."

"Then strip."

He was apprehensive. He knew what usually happened when he took his clothes off in front of a woman, but maybe it would be different, this time.

"Come on," she said. "Off with the clothes! You're makin' me really curious."

Slowly he took off his clothes, first his boots, then his shirt, then his Levi's and, finally, his underwear. He was well built, he knew that, slender but with muscles. From the look on her face as her eyes swept over him she was pleased by what she saw, and then her eyes came to his crotch . . . and everything stopped.

She stared.

"What—" he said.

"That is the dinkiest little thing I've ever seen," she said, frankly.

He didn't know what to say, but at least she wasn't

laughing. A lot of girls laughed when he took off his pants. Maybe, though, since she wasn't laughing she'd answer a question—one he'd always wondered about.

"Is it really so small?" he asked. "I mean, smaller than other men?"

"Oh honey," she said, dropping to her knees to get a better look. "Yeah, I'm afraid it is."

"Maybe," he said, "if you touched it . . ."

"Why ain't it hard, yet?" she asked. "I mean, usually by the time I get a man up here he's as hard as a randy steer."

"Well," he said, licking his lips nervously, "if you touched it . . ."

"Can I?" she asked. "Are you sure it won't break or, like, come off or something?"

He closed his eyes. He was starting to feel the shame, which he knew was always followed by the anger . . .

"Please," he said, but he wasn't pleading with her to touch him. He was pleading with himself to stay on control.

"Honey," she said, "I don't know. I mean, I need a man who's—well. Normal sized. After all, I'm a lot of woman."

She stood up and backed away from him.

"Dixie—"

"I can't do this, honey," she said. "I mean, you're good-looking enough and you've got a nice body, but sweetie, I'm afraid you got shortchanged in one real important area. You better get dressed and cover that thing up."

He might have remained in control if she hadn't continued to prance around naked in front of him. He wanted her, wanted to touch her, didn't have any idea why he was so small or why he didn't get hard right away, didn't see why he should be blamed . . .

"Dixie."

"Uh-uh, honey," she said, "I'm sorry, but that . . . that . . ." She indicated his crotch with a few flicks of her index finger. ". . . little thing just ain't gonna do it for me."

"Don't . . ." he said.

"I mean, I never seen one that small—"

"Please . . ."

She leaned over to look at it again.

"I mean, I got to squint. . . ."

As she started to straighten back up he reached out and grabbed her by the hair with one hand and by the throat with the other.

"Hey! Leggo—" but her cries were choked off by the strength in his hand.

"You shouldn't . . . make . . . fun," he said.

He turned and forced her down on the bed. As her face began to redden and she made gurgling noses all of a sudden—just like always—he was getting hard.

"I'll show you," he said, spreading her legs with his other hand, "I'll show you . . ."

He slid into her easy enough. She'd been ready even before they got to her room, and was still wet enough for easy entry.

"Honey—" she gasped. "It's okay—it's okay—" She tugged at his hand and he released the pressure enough for her to talk. "Mmm, baby," she said, "that really feels good. Give it to me, baby."

Dixie knew what she had to do. She had to fuck this weird guy and get him out of her room, and then make sure she was never alone with him again.

"Aw, honey, come on, bite me too while you're doin' that, lick me, come on, bite 'em—"

Markus didn't hear her after that. He was mindless in his quest for his own pleasure, pounding away at her now that he was rock hard. So what if he wasn't big. What was the difference?

Dixie, meanwhile, satisfied that he had let go of her throat, was wondering what he was doing down there. Was he in her? She could hardly feel a thing.

Then suddenly he was grunting and making those faces men made when they shot off into her, but she still wasn't feeling anything. This was so strange . . .

He slumped onto her, pinning her with his weight, and she said, "Okay, honey, you got to go now . . ."

"Wait—" he said.

"That was really good," she said, into his ear. "Mmm, baby, you really did it to me, but you gotta go now—"

"I . . . said . . . wait!" Markus reared up onto his knees and grabbed her by the throat again. She couldn't fool him. He knew what she was thinking, and he was going to teach her . . .

He shook his head and looked around. He was still sitting at the fire and the others were all still asleep. It had happened again. It had taken him days to finally decide to go to her room with her, because he'd been afraid of what might happen, but her breasts had just been so big, and he was so curious.

It had been okay until she had him undress. If she had just let him touch her with his clothes still on, it would have been perfect. Or if she had put the light out first . . .

Of course he couldn't send her stage fare, because he'd left her dead in her bed, her eyes open, her big breasts flattened and she didn't look so good anymore, so he really wouldn't have wanted to send her any money anyway, not given the way she looked when he left her room . . .

It just would have been a waste.

NINETEEN

Clint woke the next morning to the smell of fresh coffee. He'd relieved Damien and, in turn, had been relieved by Joe Bags. When he was able to open his eyes he saw Bags standing above him, holding out a cup of coffee.

"Thanks," he said, accepting it.

"Some of them pulled out already."

"What? Who?"

"About four of our shopkeepers woke up and had the urge to head back to Abilene."

Clint looked around. There were some men milling around, but not as many as the day before.

"Did you try to stop them?"

"No," Bags said.

"Why not?"

"What good are they to me if they don't want to be here?" Bags asked. "They'd more than likely get themselves, or somebody else, killed."

"Can't argue with that," Clint said, getting to his feet and starting to work on the coffee.

Across the camp the other storekeepers were watching them.

"You can see it happening," Bags said.

"You know," Clint said, "the three of us would move a lot faster without all of them."

"They are slowin' us down, aren't they?'

"And we might as well get it over with," Clint said, "don't you think?"

"Yes, I do."

"Before we do anything, though," Clint said, "let's check with Damien."

"Why him?"

"Because if they all leave," Clint said, "it *will* be just the three of us, and I'd like to make sure he's agreeable, as well."

"Well," Bags said, "that does sound fair."

"I'll talk to him."

Bags nodded and studied the other men while Clint went off to find Damien.

When Markus woke Mike Paul and Ray Hogan had already saddled their horses.

"What's their hurry?" he asked Carl Bankhead, the man nearest to him.

"Don't know," Bankhead said, "and I don't care."

"Maybe they're nervous," Markus said.

"They didn't ever belong with us anyway, Ralph," Bankhead said. "Too stupid."

"How smart do you have to be to take orders, Carl?"

"Smarter than those two," Bankhead said.

"Well," Markus responded, "we better make sure they leave here and go in separate directions."

"Why does it matter?" Bankhead asked. "They're bound to meet up again, anyway."

"Well," Markus said, "let's get them started in the right direction, anyway, huh?"

Bankhead made a face but said, "Okay."

Damien was in total agreement with Clint and Bags.

"We'll move twice as fast without them," Damien said. "They would only have come in handy if we found ourselves outgunned."

"I don't think that's going to happen, do you?" Clint asked.

"No," Damien said. "I expect the robbers to separate after they split up the money."

"Right," Clint said. "So I'll go and tell Bags and he can send them on their ways."

"Let's make sure we keep whatever supplies they got," Damien suggested.

"Good point," Clint said.

Hogan rode east and Paul west, while Markus, Bankhead and Ruben Sierra watched them. As for Lonnie Fields, he was still asleep.

"Should we wake him?" Sierra asked. "Or perhaps let him wake to find us all gone."

Markus and Bankhead look at him.

"A little joke, eh?"

"Carl has no sense of humor, Ruben," Markus said, "remember?"

Bankhead continued to stare at the Mexican.

"Madre mia," Sierra said, shaking his head.

"Wake him up, Carl," Markus said, "and we'll send him on his way, too."

"Right."

• • •

Clint, Bags and Damien watched the storekeepers leave. They had complained about having to leave their supplies behind, and also about not getting their money back, but it was plain on their faces that they were relieved to be going home where they wouldn't have to face any murderous bank robbers.

"Tell the mayor he'd better name somebody to take my place, temporarily," Bags said.

"You ain't comin' back?" one of the men asked.

"Not until I find those men and get back the money," Bags said.

"We wish you luck, Marshal," another man said. "We wish all three of you luck. We really do."

"Yeah," Bags said, "I believe you."

The storekeepers rode off and then Clint, Bags and Damien looked at each other.

"Let's have some breakfast and get moving," Clint finally suggested.

"And now," Damien said, "we can really move."

Lonnie Fields wanted to stay with somebody—*anybody*. In the end Markus agreed to let the youngest of the group ride with him.

"Just for a while," he added.

"Thanks, Ralph."

Bankhead and Sierra mounted up. The Mexican was going to go south, wanting to head home. Bankhead said he was going north, to Minnesota.

"What about you and the kid, Ralph?" Bankhead said.

"I'm not sure yet," Markus said. "Me and the kid will have to talk about it. Meanwhile, you two get on your way."

They shook hands with Markus, and with each other, then mounted up and rode out.

"Get your saddlebags, kid," Markus said, "we're movin' out."

"I thought we was gonna talk about where we're goin'?"

"I know where we're goin'," Markus said. "I just didn't want anybody else to."

TWENTY

Clint, Bags and Damien did, indeed, move much faster without the posse of townsmen. They reached the bank robbers' campfire before it had grown cold.

"Made up some time, looks like," Damien said, hold his hand over the remnants of the fire. "Ain't even two hours behind them."

"That's the good news," Clint said.

"What's the bad news?" Bags asked,

Damien stood up and looked at Clint, who nodded.

"Bad news is they split up," Damien said to Bags. "Went five different ways."

"Five?" Bags asked. "There was six of them."

Damien shrugged.

"Anybody fire any shots at them durin' the robbery?" he asked.

"No," Bags said, "no one."

"So one of them didn't die," Damien said. "Looks like two of them chose to stay together."

"But which two?" Bags asked.

"We don't have any way of knowing that."

"All right," Bags said. "We'll each have to pick a trail and follow it. Once we catch up to one maybe they can tell us where the others went."

"It would be my guess that one wouldn't know where the other was going," Clint said, "but this is as good a plan as any."

"I'll take the trail that goes south," Damien said.

"I'll take the trail made by two men," Bags said.

"Why that one?" Clint asked.

"I think one of them is Markus, the leader," he said. "The one who shot Alex."

"What makes you think that?"

"One of the gang members was younger than the others," Bags said. "I think he'd want to stay with his leader a while longer."

"All right," Clint said. "I'll take one of the other trails. I'll go north, I guess. As long as he doesn't take me all the way to Minnesota."

"What's wrong with Minnesota?' Damien asked. "More ghosts?"

Clint shivered and said, "It's just too damn cold."

They all mounted up and then faced each other.

"We'll have to end up back here to pick up the other trails," Clint said. "Anybody who gets back leave some kind of a message."

"Like what?" Bags asked.

"Stick a note under a rock," Clint said, "or draw an arrow in the ground to let the others know what trail you picked up."

"Okay," Bags said. "We shouldn't have to go too far to catch up with them."

"Damien?" Clint said, holding out his rifle.

"I've got some extra knives," Damien said, declining.
"Okay," Clint said. "Suit yourself."
"Let's get this done," Bags said, and they all went their separate ways.

TWENTY-ONE

Damien didn't have to be a very good tracker to stay on the trail of Ruben Sierra. The Mexican decided that they had gotten away scot-free with the money from the Abilene bank, and was not worried about someone being on his trail. For this reason he led Damien right to the town of Hutchison, Kansas, where there was a woman Sierra wanted to impress with his newfound wealth. He could make the trip home to Mexico to see his wife and children later.

For now, he had some celebrating to do.

Damien followed the trail right to Hutchison and sat his horse outside of town, surprised that the bank robber was not taking more care in his flight. Then again, maybe the man wasn't fleeing because he thought he had gotten away with no problem.

It was Damien's job to prove him wrong.

Carl Bankhead, on the other hand, was being real careful not to stop in any towns along the way. He had enough supplies to ration out so that he wouldn't need to stop until after he'd crossed the border and gotten out of Kansas. He wasn't wanted for anything in Nebraska.

Not yet, anyway.

Clint was able to comfortably follow the trail left by Bankhead, even though the man was not being as careless as his Mexican partner was. He noticed that the man was steering clear of towns, which was the smart thing to do once you got yourself wanted for a crime. Even though posters would not be out for a long time on the Abilene bank robbery he was sure that telegrams would have been sent throughout the state for lawmen to be on the lookout for the bank robbers.

But with this one staying clear of towns, Clint knew he'd end up encountering the man on the trail, where a man made his own law and was responsible for enforcing it.

And he had the enforcer right on his hip.

Ralph Markus didn't know why he had agreed to keep Lonnie Fields with him, but Lonnie wasn't even twenty yet and all he wanted to do was talk all the time. It wouldn't have been so bad if he had something to talk about, but he didn't—and yet he still talked.

"Lonnie," he said, finally.

"What?"

"If you don't shut up I'm gonna put a bullet in you."

"Huh?"

"Or two bullets," Markus went on. "In fact, I just might keep firing until you do shut up."

"But—"

"Shut up."

Lonnie opened his mouth to say something else, and then closed it.

"Besides," Markus went on, "if you keep chattering like that it will be easier for someone to follow us—all they'd have to do is listen."

Lonnie thought about saying something but decided not to. Instead he just pouted.

Markus heaved a sigh of relief and said, "Well, that's better."

At least now he'd be able to do some thinking about where to go and what to do with his money.

Joe Bags had the easiest task of all, following a trail left by two men. They were riding side by side, and while they hadn't stopped in any towns along the way it didn't look as if they were steering clear of them deliberately. Perhaps when they found one that suited them they'd stop. They were traveling in a vaguely northwestern direction, which meant they could have been headed for Nebraska or for Colorado. In either case Bags hoped to catch up to them well before then.

Of course, he still wasn't sure about what he was going to do when he found them, especially if there were still two of them. He felt almost certain that Markus himself had been the man who fired into Alex while the deputy was lying on the floor, that it had been the leader who made the killing shot—but could he kill the man on sight without making sure? After all, he was still a lawman, and he couldn't just kill someone in cold blood. He was supposed to be upholding the law.

He looked down at the badge on his chest, and then reined his horse in. He took the badge off his chest and studied it for a few moments, then he lifted the flap of his shirt pocket and put the badge inside. That done he got his horse moving again. Technically, the weight of the badge was still in the same place on his shirt, but at least now the moral weight of the badge had been shifted.

He needed that, because he knew that as soon as he saw Ralph Markus he was going to do his best to put a bullet right between the man's eyes.

TWENTY-TWO

The girl Ruben Sierra was stopping in Hutchison to see was as blonde and fair as his wife was dark and black-haired. Her name was Grace, and she worked in one of Hutchison's two saloons. Sierra thought he was special in her life, but truth be told there were dozens of men who thought that. Lucky for him—or for her—that none of those others were in town when Sierra got there.

When Sierra walked into the saloon he saw her from across the room. After three children his wife, though only twenty-five, had gone to fat. She had big, bloated breasts and buttocks and there was only a hint of the pretty *chica* she had been behind her doughy cheeks and deeply sunken eyes.

Grace, however, was tall and slender, her body extremely taut. She had breasts like ripe fruit, round and firm, and a bottom almost like a boy's, but smooth and well muscled. Her hair was long and golden, her eyes green, her mouth wide and talented. The Mexican considered the blonde *gringa* to be his dream girl—but he did love his wife and his children, and intended to have more children, yet. So he settled for stopping in town and seeing Grace whenever he had the time.

When Grace saw Sierra enter the saloon she was pleased. Not because she missed him, but because she knew that someone had walked into the saloon who would spend money on her. She ran into his arms with a squeal and he kissed her soundly. When Sierra was clean and sober he wasn't half bad to her, but he now smelled pretty bad from days on the trail.

"Ruben," she said, pushing him away, "you need a bath."

"I was in too much of a hurry to see you, *chica*," he said, pinching her cheek. "You are as beautiful as ever."

"And you as charming," she said, "but you still smell like a horse, Ruben. A sweaty horse."

"I will go and bathe for you, *cariño mio*," he said. "I will go to the barbershop."

"And I will wait for you here," she said. "I'll have a cold beer waiting for you when you return."

"I will return quickly," Sierra said, "but not for the promise of a cold beer. And I have good news for you."

"I can't wait," she said, clapping her hands together.

He took her hand, kissed it and left. Grace walked over to the bar and leaned on it.

"Why do you waste your time with losers like him?" the bartender asked. It was his job to look after the girls.

"He says he has good news, Larry," she said. "Do you know what that means?"

"I got no idea."

"It means money," she said. "He came into some money."

"Probably stole it."

"I don't care how he got it," she said, "as long as he has it, and he spends it on me."

"You're a gold digger, Grace," he said.

"You're absolutely right, Larry," she said, without shame. "And I'm a good one."

Damien had made good time and upon entering Hutchison did not bother to take his horse to the livery stable. Instead he went to check out the saloons in town, figuring that was the first place the bank robber would go. He happened to be in the saloon when Grace went squealing into Sierra's arms, although he didn't know who either one of them was. The man, however, had obviously been on the trail a long time. When the woman sent him off to take a bath Damien went to the bar and leaned against it. From his vantage point he heard the conversation between the girl and the bartender, a conversation that convinced him that Mexican who was off taking a bath was one of the Abilene bank robbers.

"Get you somethin'?"

Damien looked up to see the bartender staring at him expectantly. Why not? He had a little time. He wanted the Mexican to be very involved with his bath over at the barbershop.

"I'll have a beer," he said. He didn't tell the bartender that it would be a quick one.

When Ruben Sierra went into the back of the barbershop, where the bathtubs were, he had his saddlebags with him. He was going to keep his money very close to him the whole time he was in town. And he was smart. He would tell no one about it except for Grace.

He made sure that his water was the right temperature for him—tepid, never hot. He hated hot baths. Once the water was right he got into the tub with the saddlebags and his gunbelt on a chair next to it, both within easy reach. He began to soap himself, staring happily down at his penis, which was already erect in anticipation of the time he would spend with Grace.

Damien finished his beer and sauntered over to the barbershop.

"Be right with you," the barber said, "soon as I finish this fella up."

"No hurry," Damien said. "Mexican come in here looking for a bath?"

The barber looked at him.

"Yeah, he's in the back."

"Anybody else?"

"No, just him."

"Thanks."

As Damien started the barber asked, "Is there gonna be trouble?"

Damien thought a moment, then said, "I guess that'll depend on him."

He went through the back doors and headed in the direction of the splashing.

TWENTY-THREE

Clint had the advantage of riding Eclipse, the Darley Arabian stallion who had been a gift from P. T. Barnum when he was in New York. While Eclipse was not Duke, Clint's old black gelding who he had been forced to put out to pasture, he was the second best horse Clint had ever ridden. He made good time pushing the stallion, and before long he could see a rider off in the distance. There was no way to be sure that this was one of the bank robbers, except for one—he had to catch up to him and ask him.

Carl Bankhead was looking for a place to camp when something—he didn't know what—made him look over his shoulder. In the distance he saw a rider. He couldn't recognize him, but he didn't think it was any of his partners. Whoever it was, he was just riding along leisurely like, didn't look like he was in any hurry. He could have been a posse man, but that didn't seem likely to Bankhead, either. Still, he decided to keep on going a bit longer and see if the man stuck with him.

• • •

Joe Bags had an advantage over Clint and Damien in that he had seen almost all of the bank robbers at one time or another while they were in town. He felt sure he'd be able to recognize any of the six of them. He also knew that fate would not play a cruel trick on him. He felt sure that at the end of the trail he was following he'd find Ralph Markus and one other of the robbers, probably the young one they called Lonnie.

Idly, as he continued to follow the clear trail, he wondered how the others were doing.

"Where are we headed, Ralph?" Lonnie asked. He thought he could ask a question at this point because he'd kept quiet for a while.

"A little town I know of," Markus said. "Friend of mine lives there and we'll be able to check the news comin' out of Abilene. Give us some idea of who may be huntin' us, or how many."

"Sounds good," Lonnie said, and then fell silent.

Markus almost felt bad about shutting Lonnie up. Kind of felt like he'd kicked a puppy. He almost started talking to Lonnie himself, just to make up for it, but he decided not to. Why ruin a good thing?

TWENTY-FOUR

Damien moved down the hall carefully, not wanting the Mexican to hear him coming. He needn't have bothered, though, since Ruben Sierra was singing happily in his native language and at the top of his lungs. In fact, he wasn't aware of Damien at all until he saw him standing in the open doorway.

"Hey, *cabrón*," he said, "can't you see this bathtub is taken? Try the next one."

"I kinda like this one," Damien said.

"Eh? Oh, you are a *maricón*? Is that it? Well, my friend, I like women very much so you will not find any satisfaction here. So go away, before I take my gun and give you a new asshole, eh?"

Damien looked at the saddlebags on the chair, and the gunbelt hanging on the back of it.

"Those saddlebags look mighty full," Damien said. "What have you got in there?"

"That is none of your business," Sierra said. He dropped the soap into the tub and rinsed his hands. It was bad enough he would have to try for his gun with wet hands; he didn't need them, to be soapy, as well.

"Take my advice, amigo," he said, "turn around and leave."

"No," Damien said, "I think I need to take a look inside those saddlebags, friend."

"And what exactly would you be lookin' for, eh?"

"Money."

Sierra's eyes narrowed.

"How much money?"

"A lot."

"What makes you think I have a lot of money?"

"Because you and your friends stole it from the Bank of Abilene just yesterday," Damien said, "and I don't think you've had time to spend very much of it."

"*Señor*," Sierra said, "you are a lawman?

"No."

"A posse man, then?"

"That's right."

"But you have no gun."

"I don't need one."

"Dios mio," Sierra said, "they have sent a crazy man after me?"

"Not so crazy," Damien said. "Now, let me explain it to you before you try for your gun, amigo."

"What is there to explain?"

"All I want is the money," Damien said. "We know it wasn't you who shot the deputy from what the witnesses said. If you let me have the money, I'll let you go. Oh, and one other thing."

"And what is that?"

"I'd like to know where your *compadres* went."

"Alas," Sierra said, "that I do not know. If I did, maybe I would tell you, just to get rid of you. But . . . I do not."

"And the money?"

Sierra shook his head sadly.

"I cannot give that to you. I have worked too hard for it."

"The people who put the money in the bank worked hard for it," Damien said. "You and your friends just stole it."

"Stealing is hard work, believe me," Sierra said, "I have been doing it a long time."

"Well," Damien said, "I don't have any more time to talk. I'll just take the money and be on my way."

"My friend," Sierra said, 'one step toward my saddlebags will be your last."

"Let's find out."

Damien took a step and the Mexican went for his gun. Before he could grab it, though, something punched him in the chest. He looked down and was shocked to see the hilt of a knife protruding. The entire blade was inside of him. Blood gushed from his mouth then, and as the water began to turn red the light of life dimmed in his eyes and he was gone.

TWENTY-FIVE

The sheriff of Hutchison tossed Damien's knife onto his desk and then put him in a cell. Then he stood outside the cell with his arms folded and a confused look on his face.

"You don't have a badge but you claim to be part of a posse," the lawman said.

"When you form a posse, Sheriff, do you deputize everyone in it?"

"I do."

"Give them all badgcs?"

The sheriff frowned.

"I don't have enough of them to go around."

"Exactly. Look, you saw the money in the man's suitcase," Damien said. "Where do you think he got all that money?"

"I don't know," the sheriff said, "but I aim to find out. Meanwhile, I'll just keep you in here until I do."

"Just remember, Sheriff," Damien said, "it was me who came to you."

"That," said Sheriff Harold V. Davis, Jr., "is what's got me confused, friend."

"There it is, up ahead," Markus said.

"What's it called?" Lonnie asked.

"Baskerville."

"What kind of name is that?"

"Damned if I know," Markus said, "but that's what the town is called. Come on, let's go. I'm hungry for some hot food."

"So am I!"

Bankhead knew he had to camp soon. His horse was growing tired. The rider was still behind him, not gaining, but not losing ground. Not chasing, he decided, but possibly following.

He decided he was going to have to do something about it.

Clint knew he'd been spotted. There wasn't much he could have done to avoid it. He wanted to keep the man in view, and he knew that would also put him in the man's view. If the fellow was innocent he wouldn't care that there was someone riding behind him. If he was guilty, maybe he'd try to find out why Clint was there.

Of course, he could have been guilty of something without being guilty of robbing the bank in Abilene—but that remained to be seen.

Joe Bags had never been to this part of the state, so he didn't really know where he was headed. He hoped it was a town, though. If it was, he might be able to get some help from the local law in taking Markus and the other robber he had with him. His anger at the death of Alex McCord was becoming tempered by the fact that he was going to have to go against two men. Sure, he wanted to avenge the death of the young deputy, but he didn't want to die himself while doing it.

First thing he'd do when he got to the next town was hook up with the local law and see how much help he could get. With a couple of guns behind him maybe Ralph Markus wouldn't be in such a hurry to shoot it out.

Damien waited in his cell calmly. He'd done his job, now all he needed was for the sheriff to do his. If Davis sent a telegram to Abilene everything would be explained to him, and Damien would be out of the cell. Once he was out he needed a bath and some hot food, and a beer. Then, after a good night's sleep, he could get back on the job, retrace his steps and pick up another man's trail.

Sheriff Harold Davis accepted the telegram from the clerk and scanned it quickly.

"Is that what you were waitin' for, Sheriff?" the man asked.

"Looks like it," Davis said. "Says here the bank in Abilene was robbed and the sheriff went out with a posse to track the robbers down."

"Also says a deputy was killed."

"I can see that," Davis said. He folded the telegram and stuffed it into his pocket.

"Looks like you're gonna have ta let that feller out of your jail," the clerk said.

"Looks like it," the lawman said. "Thanks, Dave."

Sheriff Davis left the telegraph office and made a

stop at the café on his way to the jail. He was hungry, and he figured the posse man must be, too. Might as well bring a little peace offering with him when he let the fella out.

TWENTY-SIX

Clint topped a rise, and the rider ahead of him was no longer in sight. Obviously, the man had decided to make a move. Clint had two choices. He could lay back and see how patient the man was, or he could ride forward and see what the fella had in mind. Short of being shot in the back Clint felt sure he would be able to handle whatever the man had.

He gave Eclipse his head and started down.

Bankhead waited for the rider to go past him, then stepped out and called, "Hold it right there."

The rider stopped and froze.

"Why are you following me?"

"You mind if I turn around and see who I'm talking to?" Clint Adams asked.

"Turn slowly," Bankhead said, "and keep your hand away from your gun."

"You're the boss, friend."

Clint turned and saw Bankhead standing there with his gun out and pointed at him. He swallowed once, realizing the man could have shot him in the back if he'd wanted to. But he'd taken that chance and had come out of it okay.

So far.

"No hard feelings, I hope," Sheriff Davis said to Damien.

"This more than makes up for it, Sheriff," Damien said. "Some of the best damn beef stew I ever had."

"My daughter is the cook," the man said. "She owns the café."

The sheriff had come back to the jail and had released Damien, returning his knife. Damien had smelled the food even before he saw the two trays on the man's desk.

"One of them for me?"

The sheriff nodded. "By way of apology."

"You don't need to apologize for doin' your job, Sheriff," Damien said, "but I'll gladly accept the food."

So the two men had sat down and started eating together, seated across the desk from each other.

"You're pretty good with a knife if you took a man with a gun," the sheriff said.

"I don't like guns," Damien said. "Too noisy."

"Well," Davis said, "I guess when you're as good as you are with a knife you can worry about things like that. Where you headed after this?'

"Back to where I picked up this fella's trail," Damien said. "I'm workin' with the marshal and Clint Adams—"

"Adams? The Gunsmith? He's in on this?"

"He sure is," Damien said. "Him and the marshal are friends."

"And it's just the three of you?" Davis asked. "The

telegram I got from Abilene said there was over a dozen in the posse."

"There was, but the storekeepers went back to town. There's just the three of us now."

"Huntin' how many?"

"Six, but they split up. Now that I found this one I got to go lookin' for another. By the way, I'll need those saddlebags full of money."

"I got it right here." The sheriff leaned down and brought the saddlebags up from beneath his desk. "A lot of money in here."

"I guess."

"You know how much?"

"Nope."

"Ain't you curious?"

Damien took the saddlebags off the desk and placed on the floor by his feet.

"My job is to bring it back," he said, "not to count it."

"Sure wish I could go with you," Davis said, "but my days in the saddle trackin' outlaws are over. Reached fifty last year, and I'm feelin' every minute of it, these days."

"You got a job to do here," Damien said, stuffing the last piece of biscuit soaked in stew into his mouth. "Mighty fine meal, Sheriff. My compliments to your daughter. I got to be goin'."

He picked up the saddlebags and stood up.

"Stayin' the night?" Davis asked.

"No," Damien said, "I got to get back."

"In the dark?"

"I see real good in the dark. I just got to make my way back to where I started, and camp until daylight. Lucky it didn't take me long to catch up to this fella."

"By the way," Davis said, walking to the door with Damien, "what should we do with him?"

"Plant him I guess," Damien said. "I don't much care."

"Put him in potter's field, I guess," Davis said. "Didn't have nothin' on him that told us his name."

"Check with a yellow-haired gal over at the saloon," Damien said. "She looked real glad to see him when he walked in."

"There's a couple of gals fit that description over there," Davis said. "I'll ask."

"Much obliged, Sheriff," Damien said, extending his hand.

Davis shook it and said, "Again, I'm sorry I put you in my pokey."

"Doin' your job, Sheriff," Damien said, going out the door, "same as I'm doin' mine."

TWENTY-SEVEN

"I'm waitin' to hear why you're on my trail," Bankhead said to Clint.

"What makes you think I am?"

"You been behind me for the past I don't know how many miles," Bankhead said. "Makin' my back itch."

"You got a guilty conscience?"

"Mister," Bankhead said, "you're under the gun right now, so I think you just better answer my questions the way I ask 'em."

Clint sat easily on his horse, keeping loose. The man didn't look ready to shoot, yet.

"Mind if I step down while you're asking?"

"Yeah, I mind. Where are you from?"

"Originally," Clint asked, "or lately?"

"Let's try lately."

"Well," Clint said, "recently I passed through Abilene—hey, they had a bank robbery over there yesterday. I don't suppose you'd know anything about that?"

"Now why would I know anything about a bank robbery?"

Clint shrugged.

"Maybe you were passing through, like me," Clint said, "or maybe—hey, you wouldn't be one of those fellas, would you? That why you're so nervous?"

"Mister," Bankhead said, "you ask too many questions for your own good."

"Big fault of mine," Clint said, "asking questions. But you know what?"

"What?"

"I'm going to take that as a yes."

Suddenly, Clint just slipped out of the saddle as if he were falling. He dropped off his horse to the left, hoping that a stray bullet wouldn't hit Eclipse. He'd decided that this man was one of the bank robbers, and he couldn't count on him to just talk much longer.

As he dropped to the ground he drew his gun. While the man was trying to see him around the horse Clint fired from beneath the horse. His first bullet struck the man in the hip, spinning him around. Clint rushed to his feet and slapped Eclipse on the rump so he'd run off, away from the action.

As Clint got to his feet Bankhead had fallen and dropped his gun. It lay a few feet from him and he started to reach for it.

"Don't!" Clint shouted, and the man froze.

Bankhead stopped and looked at him.

"Who are you?"

"My name's Clint Adams."

It was obvious the man knew the name.

"This is about Abilene?"

"That's right."

"What's it to you?" Bankhead asked. "You didn't have no money in that bank."

"The marshal's a friend of mine," Clint said, "and I happened to like that deputy you killed."

"I didn't kill no deputy," Bankhead said. "That crazy Mexican shot him, and then Markus finished him. I had nothin' to do with that."

"Doesn't matter," Clint said. "I'm talking you back to stand trial for bank robbery and murder. Where's your share of the money?"

"In my saddlebags," Bankhead said, grimacing from the pain in his hip. "You can have it. Just let me go."

"You'd bleed to death before you got very far."

"I'll take my chances," Bankhead said. "Better that than prison, or the end of a rope."

"Sorry," Clint said, "but you don't have enough money in your saddlebags to buy your way out of this."

"You don't even know how much I got!"

"It doesn't matter," Clint said.

Bankhead stared at Clint, then licked his lips and looked over at his gun lying in the dirt.

"Don't try it," Clint said.

Bankhead looked at Clint and said, "I got to."

He lunged . . .

TWENTY-EIGHT

When they rode into Baskerville and got to the livery Markus told Lonnie Fields to go to the hotel.

"Get two rooms."

"How long we gonna be stayin'?"

"I don't know," Markus said. "One or two nights."

"Ain't that dangerous?" Lonnie asked. "We still ain't that far from Abilene, ya know."

"I know, Lonnie," Markus said. "They'd never expect us to actually stop in a town this close."

"But . . ."

"But what?"

"What about the sheriff here?" the younger man asked. "What if he heard about the robbery?"

"I'm hoping he did," Markus said.

"Huh?"

"Remember I told you I had a friend here?"

"Yeah."

"It's the sheriff."

Markus hoisted his saddlebags containing his share of

the money—and the extra three hundred and eighty-something dollars—and started for the sheriff's office.

"You look comfortable."

Sheriff Cal Eldred looked up at the sound of the voice and saw Ralph Markus standing in the doorway.

"Be damned," he said. "You did the Abilene job, didn't you?"

Markus walked to the desk and put his saddlebags down on top of it. He dug out three hundred and eighty dollars and put it on the desk.

"What's that for?" Eldred asked.

"I owe you."

"For what?"

"Information," the bank robber said. "What did you hear about the Abilene job?"

The sheriff hesitated a moment, then picked up the money and dug a telegram out of his pocket. He gave it to Markus, who read it. It informed the sheriff that the Markus gang had held up the Abilene bank and killed a deputy. It also said that about a dozen-man posse was on their trail, and they might be headed his way.

"Why'd you kill the deputy?" Eldred asked.

"That crazy Mexican did it," Markus said. "The deputy came in to make a deposit. The Mexican wanted his money and he wouldn't give it up. Just a crazy coincidence."

"Nobody else fired?"

Markus shook his head.

"Witnesses'll say the Mex did it."

"You plan on holing up here?"

"No," Markus said, "just wanted a stopover to find out what information was coming out of Abilene. Probably leave in the morning."

"Good," Eldred said. He was older than Markus by a good dozen years or so, and had been more a friend of the family than of his. "Out of respect for your mom and dad I won't run you out."

Yeah, sure, Markus thought, *and because of the three hundred and eighty dollars.* This was one tin star that could be bought cheap.

"We'll be on our way."

"We?" the sheriff asked. "The Mex is with you?"

"No," Markus said, "kid named Lonnie Fields. You don't know him."

"And I don't want to," Eldred said. "Be all right with me if you both left without me seein' you in the mornin'."

"Count on it."

Markus picked up his saddlebags and walked to the door. He left without saying another word.

Sheriff Eldred sat back in his chair and counted the money Markus had given him.

Joe Bags had made good time. The tracks looked fresh to him as he rode into town, if he was properly applying the quick tracking lessons Damien had given him the day before.

He rode to the livery, dismounted and went inside.

"Help ya?" the livery man asked.

"Two riders just came in."

"That's right, a little while ago," the man said. He was in his sixties and squinted at Bags to see him clearly. "What's it to ya?"

Bags took his badge out of his pocket and held it where the man could see it clearly.

"Marshal of where?"

"Abilene."

"Big bank robbery there yesterday."

"I know."

"Them two the ones what done it?"

"Two of them, anyway."

"One of them went to the hotel," the man said. "Don't know where the other one went."

"Much obliged. Who's the sheriff of this town?"

"Cal Eldred."

"What's he like?"

"Like everybody else in this pissant town," the man said. "Marking time."

Might not be much help, then, but it was worth a try.

"Okay, thanks. Take care of my horse, will you?"

"How long?"

"I'm not sure," Bags said. "I'll let you know."

As Bags tucked his badge back into his pocket and walked away the old livery man shook his head and doubted that he'd be seeing that marshal again . . . alive.

TWENTY-NINE

Bags took his badge out of his pocket and showed it to Sheriff Eldred.

"Why aren't you wearing' it?"

Bags put it back in his pocket.

"It's a long story."

"How do I know it's yours?"

"Check with Abilene if you like," Bags said. "Or look at my shirt. There are plenty of little holes here where the badge usually goes."

"Naw," Eldred said, "I believe you. What brings you to Baskerville?"

"I'm tracking a band of bank robbers," Bags said. "The Markus gang? Maybe you heard about the robbery in Abilene? They killed my deputy while they were at it."

"That's too bad."

"Yeah, it is," Bags said. "He was very young."

"What makes you think they're here?"

"Two of them are here," Bags said. "I know it. I followed their trail all the way to the livery."

"You must be a pretty good tracker."

"I get by."

"Have you spotted them yet?"

"I came to see you first."

"Well," Eldred said, rubbing his jaw, "I haven't seen any stranger in town today, but then I still got rounds to make. Why don't you get comfortable in the hotel and—"

"I don't want to get too comfortable, Sheriff," Joe Bags said. "I think I'll just go along with you on your rounds."

"Well . . . if that's what you want to do."

"That's what I want to do."

The sheriff grabbed his hat and stood up.

"Will you recognize these boys when you see them?"

"They were in Abilene for a while before they hit the bank," Bags said. "I've got every face memorized."

That was what Cal Eldred was afraid of.

Damien rode in the dark until he got back to the cold campfire left by the Markus gang, from where the tracks all started. He hoped that when daylight came the other trails would still be there. Somebody could have come by in the meanwhile and trampled them.

He was very careful not to trample what was left as he built the fire up once again. He staked his horse away from the camp for that purpose.

Using a coffeepot he always kept in his saddlebags he brewed a pot and took out some beef jerky to stave off his hunger. He was nodding off at the fire when he heard a sound that brought him completely awake: a snapping sound of a man or a horse stepping on a twig.

"Hello by the fire!" a voice called seconds later. It sounded like Clint Adams.

"Come ahead!"

Clint walked Eclipse into the camp, also wanting to be careful not to trample any tracks.

"I was hoping it might be you or Bags when I smelled the coffee," he said. "Get your man?"

"I did," Damien said. "He's dead, but I got his saddlebags with his share in them."

"So I did," Clint said, "and my man is dead, too."

"Mine was a Mexican," Damien said, "nothing on him to give a name, though. The sheriff in Hutchison will have it, though, if it's important. My horse is out there, away from the tracks. Put yours with him and I'll pour you a cup of coffee and break you off a piece of jerky. We can exchange stories."

"I'll be right back for that coffee."

They sat around the fire, first Damien and then Clint relaying what had happened.

"This is pure luck, you know," Damien said, afterward.

"What is?"

"Catching up to them so soon, and still in Kansas. I wonder how the marshal is doin'?"

"I was thinking about that, too," Clint said. "He chose the trail made by two horses. I couldn't talk him into leaving that one for last."

"Well, we got two more trails to follow—I hope. Long as nobody came along today and trampled 'em."

"I wonder if Markus will stop in a town nearby," Clint said.

"That'd be stupid."

"Or smart," Clint said. "He'd think that we wouldn't expect it, and from there he could get some information out of Abilene."

"Think he's that smart?"

"I don't know," Clint said. "I kind of hope not."

"Why?"

"If he is that smart, and he stops in a town, Bags is going to catch up to him."

"Can't he handle himself?"

"Against two men, maybe," Clint said.

"He could get help from the local law."

"I hope that's the case, Damien," Clint said. "I hope so."

It was dark by the time Bags and Sheriff Eldred finished the man's rounds.

"Didn't see them huh?" Eldred asked.

"No, but they could be in the hotel," Bags said. "I'll check there."

"Look," the sheriff said, "we got to eat and they won't be going anywhere. Let me take you to a little café and then after we eat I'll go to the hotel with you. Whataya say?"

Bags hesitated, but then his stomach began gnawing at him.

"Okay," he said, "you're on."

"It's just down the street," Eldred said. "You go and get a table and order us a couple steaks. I just got to stop by my office for a minute."

"Fine," Bags said. "I'll see you there."

Eldred watched as Bags walked off down the street and then he turned and headed not for his office, but for the hotel.

THIRTY

"Set a watch?" Damien asked.

"What for?" Clint asked. "They're nowhere near here, and we're both going to need to be rested."

"It's okay," Damien said. "I sleep light."

Clint looked up at the moon and said, "Too early to turn in anyway. I'm going to clean my gun."

Damien watched as Clint set out a cloth and began to take his weapon apart and clean it.

"It ain't just a name with you, is it?" he asked. "Gunsmith, I mean. You know what you're doin'."

"I know my way around guns," Clint said.

"Well, that there's one of the things I like about knives," Damien said. "I can just wipe my knife on my pants if I want, and it's clean."

"You've got a point."

"And I never have to worry about it not working."

"Another point."

"What do you like about guns?"

"I'm good with them," Clint said. "I'm not good with a knife at all."

"Good enough reason."

"You must be pretty damn good to take a man with a gun," Clint said.

"It's all in the motion," Damien said, taking out his knife. "One fluid motion, no need to cock a hammer or squeeze a trigger."

Clint was already putting his Colt back together again. Once that was done he cocked the hammer several times before reloading the weapon and replacing it in his holster.

"Never saw a man take a weapon apart and put it back together so fast before," Damien said.

"It becomes second nature."

"You as good with a gun as they say you are?"

Clint smiled at Damien and said, "Nobody's that good."

Damien studied him for a few moments, then said, "No, I think maybe you are."

"What makes you think that?'

" 'Cause you don't brag," Damien said. "I gave you a chancc, but you don't brag. A man who don't brag about how good he is is usually pretty damn good."

"All this talk is making me tired."

"Fine," Damien said. "We don't have to talk about how good either one of us is. Fact is we're here and the two fellas we went out after ain't. That's good enough for me."

"Me, too."

Bags waited and waited in the café, then started eating his steak. He was done with his and still the sheriff had not returned to eat his, which was sitting on the other side of the table. He finally paid the bill and left the café, stopping just outside on the boardwalk to check the street. It was a quiet town, with the only sound he could make out being a distant piano from the town's only saloon.

He stepped down into the street and started walking toward the hotel. He wondered what had happened to the sheriff? Had duty called? Had some misfortune befallen him? Some personal problem? Okay, so he'd have to go and check on Markus on his own. If that's the way it had to be, that was his job, wasn't it? It's what he was out here to do?

He wondered how Clint and Damien had fared in their chases? Better than he had, he hoped.

He came within sight of the hotel and slowed his pace. All he had to do was show his badge and check the register. Would they have signed in under their real names, he wondered? He just had to determine that two strangers *had* checked in, get their room numbers and, if they were in their rooms, he could take them one at a time.

As he got closer to the hotel he realized there was a man sitting in a chair out in front. He wondered if it was the sheriff.

"Sheriff?" he called.

The man didn't answer.

Bags dropped his hand down to his gun and kept walking. It was dark out, with only one light nearby, and that was across the street. He also noticed that the lobby was dark. That should have been a giveaway, but he was still thinking that the man seated in front was the sheriff.

"Sheriff Eldred?"

Finally, he got close enough to the hotel to make out a shape, and it didn't look like the sheriff. The man stood up then and stepped forward, and his face was illuminated by a shaft of moonlight.

It was Ralph Markus.

"Lookin' for me, Marshal?" the outlaw asked.

Bags went for his gun, and even as he did he knew he was too late. He could feel it in the pit of his stomach, a combination of fear and shame that he'd been caught so easily. The shot came from behind him. Something hot punched him right between the shoulders, just below his neck. It staggered him forward a few steps and took his breath away. He caught his balance and managed not to fall. He looked up and saw Markus smiling at him from the boardwalk. He tried to get his gun out.

"Stubborn," Ralph Markus said. He drew his gun and shot Joe Bags in the face.

The marshal of Abilene was dead before he hit the ground.

THIRTY-ONE

Clint woke the next morning to find Damien sitting by the fire, making coffee.

"Did you sleep?" he asked.

"Yes," Damien said, "I don't need much. Coffee?"

"Thanks."

Damien handed him a cup then poured one for himself.

"I took a look around," he said. "There is still enough of a trail to follow. One goes east, the other west."

"I've been thinking about that."

"About what?"

"What to do about these trails," Clint said. "I've got a bad feeling."

"About what?"

"About Bags going after those two alone," Clint said.

"What do you want to do?"

"I want to go after him."

"And what do you want me to do?"

"Take the other trails."

"Both of them?"

"If you can."

Damien shrugged.

"I don't see why not. You think the marshal is on the trail of Markus himself?"

"Yeah, I do," Clint said.

"I could come with you and help," Damien said. "I can pick up those other trails any time."

"No," Clint said, "we want to get them before they go too far, before they spend the money. You track the other two and I'll follow Bags. I think he's going to need help."

"Whatever you say," Damien said. "You're the boss."

"Why is that?"

Damien shrugged. " 'Cause I don't wanna be," he said. "Bein' the boss ain't no fun for me, Clint. I just like to do what I'm told."

"Well, I'm not telling you, Damien," Clint said. "All I'm doing is suggesting a course of action."

"Well," Damien said, "let's do it, then."

"Okay," Clint said. "Let's douse this fire and get moving."

Sheriff Cal Eldred was beside himself. He was sitting in his office the next morning, waiting for Ralph Markus to show up. When he did he was going to have to tell him what he thought. Markus had to leave town, or else.

He just didn't know what he would do if Markus asked, "Or else what?"

Over breakfast Lonnie asked, "That was a good shot, wasn't it?"

"It was a perfect shot, Lonnie," Markus said, "except it didn't kill him." Once again, as with Ruben Sierra shooting the deputy in the bank, Markus had to clean up after someone.

"Well, I got rid of the body, though, didn't I?"

"That you did do, kid," Markus said.

"So now we ain't gotta run no more, right?" Lonnie asked. "I mean, with that marshal taken care of?"

"Clint Adams is still out there lookin', Lonnie."

"How do you know he's lookin'?"

"Because he ain't the kind of man who gives up."

"Aw, we could take him the same way, Ralph," Lonnie said, proudly. "You and me, we make a good team, don't we?"

"Sure, kid, we make a good team," Markus said, and then added, "Except now we're goin' our separate ways."

"What? How come?"

"Because if that marshal's body is found they're really gonna be after us," Markus said. "We make smaller targets traveling separately."

"Aw, Ralph . . ." He lowered his voice. "I can't."

"Can't what?"

"Can't go it alone."

"Why not, kid?"

Lonnie wet his lips and then said, "I don't know what to do."

"Just pick a direction and keep goin'."

"Jesus, Ralph—"

"Time to grow up, Lonnie," Markus said.

"Aw, Ralph—"

"Shut up, Lonnie!" Markus said, cutting the younger man off in mid whine.

As Markus entered the sheriff's office Eldred said, "I didn't know you were gonna kill him!"

"What did you think we were gonna do, Cal?' Markus asked. "Shake his hand?"

"What do I say when they come lookin' for him?"

"Say he wasn't here," Markus answered, "say he was and he left, but don't send them in my direction, Cal. You were friends with my folks but if you send them after me I'll come back and kill you. Got it?"

"I got it."

"We're leavin' now," Markus said. "I know that's a relief to you."

"I—yeah, but—"

"But what?"

"Where's the body?"

"Don't worry about the body," Markus said, heading for the door. "It'll turn up sooner or later, and all you have to do is look surprised."

THIRTY-TWO

Clint and Damien split up, with Damien following the trail that led east. Clint was able to follow Bags's trail fairly comfortably because now it had been left by three horses.

It only took Damien a few miles to realize that the man whose trail he was following had doubled back. The way he figured it, Markus had probably wanted them all to split up, but two of them had planned to meet somewhere on their own. If he was right, then following this man's trail would lead him to the last two, and that suited him fine.

"Whataya think Ralph will say about us meetin' up?" Mike Paul asked Ray Hogan.

"Who cares?" Hogan asked. "We're probably never gonna see him again."

"You mean we ain't gonna be a gang again?"

"I get the feelin' Ralph Markus was all through with us, Mike," Hogan said. "That's why he wanted to split up."

Paul looked at his friend across their fire and asked, "So what do we do now?"

"I got an idea," Hogan said. "Why don't we start our own gang."

"Our own?'

"Yeah, the Hogan Paul gang."

He thought Paul would object but the man surprised him by saying, "That sounds good. Who do we get?"

"Let's get this fire out and get on the trail," Hogan said, "and we can talk about it while we ride."

Outside of Baskerville Ralph Markus reined in his horse and looked at Lonnie Fields.

"You're on your own, kid."

"Aw, Ralph—"

"Start ridin'," Markus said. "That way. I'm going that way." He pointed north for Lonnie, and west for himself.

"Ralph," Lonnie said, "I don't know what to do with all this money. I ain't never had this much. I—I might make a mistake. I might waste it!"

Markus studied the younger man and said, "You know, you might be right, Lonnie."

"Plus they're bound to be after us for killing that marshal," Lonnie said. "I think we're better off sticking together and watching each other's back."

"You know," Markus said, "when you're right, you're right, kid."

Lonnie brightened.

"You mean about staying together?"

"No," Markus said, drawing his gun, "about you wastin' all that money."

Wha—" Lonnie started, but he was cut off when Markus shot him in the throat.

Lonnie fell from his horse and hit the ground like a

sack of shit. Markus dismounted, walked to the other horse and removed the saddlebags full of money. He opened them and took out the extra shirt and whatever else Lonnie had in there and dropped the stuff on the ground next to the body.

"You're right, Lonnie, about them trackin' us for that marshal," Markus said, talking to the dead body. "I'm gonna need somethin' to slow them down, and you're it."

He leaned over and went through the dead man's pockets. He was glad he did. The kid had stuffed some of the cash in there. As an afterthought he took off the kid's gunbelt to take with him as an extra. He left the rifle on the saddle, and remounted, leaving the horse next to the body, figuring it would wander off sooner or later.

"You know, kid," he said to the body, "this might not have happened if you would have just learned to shut up sometimes."

Markus turned his horse and started west, heading to California, ultimately. He now had more money than he had ever dreamed off, and California sounded like a nice place to start over.

Clint followed the well worn trail to a town called Baskerville. He'd never heard of it, and was surprised that the bank robbers would even stop. Still, he and Damien *had* discussed the possibility of Markus thinking that no one would suspect such a move. Hopefully, he'd find a couple of the bank robbers there—maybe Markus himself—and Joe Bags.

He bypassed the livery, deciding instead to go right to the sheriff's office. Bags was sure to have checked in with the law first.

He dismounted outside the office and entered without knocking. A man was behind the desk, either in the act of standing or about to sit, Clint didn't know which. All he cared about was that he was wearing a badge.

"Can I help ya?" the sheriff asked.

"I'm looking for Marshal Joe Bags, from Abilene," Clint said.

"Marshal of Abilene?" the sheriff repeated. "What would he be doing here?"

"Tracking some bank robbers," Clint said. "I'm sure you heard about the robbery in Abilene."

"Oh yeah, I heard about it," the sheriff said. "That kind of news travels real fast."

"Well, I'm with the posse that was riding with the marshal," Clint said. "He tracked two of them here, and I tracked the three of them."

"Here, huh?" the man said. "You'd think he would have checked in with me on that."

"I thought he would have," Clint said. Could Bags have been hotheaded enough not to have checked in? "No strangers in town, Sheriff?"

"Not that I know of," the man said. "Maybe you followed the wrong trail here?"

Clint shook his head.

"It was the only trail to follow," Clint said. "Couldn't be mistaken."

"Well then," the lawman said, "maybe you and me ought to take a look around town and see what we can find."

He came around the desk and extended his hand.

"I'm Sheriff Cal Eldred."

"Good to meet you, Sheriff," Clint said. He took the man's hand and looked into his eyes. He was dead certain that he was being lied to. "My name is Clint Adams."

Eldred froze in mid-handshake, then took his hand back as if he had been burned.

"Clint Adams . . . the Gunsmith?"

"That's right."

Eldred took a step back.

"He didn't tell me . . ." he started, and then stopped.

"What, Sheriff?" Clint asked. "What didn't Ralph Markus tell you?"

THIRTY-THREE

Sheriff Eldred couldn't speak for a moment. His eyes darted back and forth and he licked his lips.

"Come on, Sheriff," Clint said. "It's pretty obvious that Markus was here. What is he, an old friend?"

"I was . . . friends with his parents," Eldred finally said.

"And that means you have to help their son get away with robbery and murder?" Clint asked.

"I—"

Clint held up his hand.

"I'm not looking for an explanation, Sheriff," Clint said. "I just want some answers."

The sheriff's shoulders slumped, but in truth he was happy not to have to try to explain himself.

"All right."

"Was Markus here?"

"Yes."

"With another man?"

"Yes."

"And where are they now?"

"I don't know."

"Sheriff—"

"I swear, they left this mornin'."

"And what about the marshal?"

"He . . . left also, followin' them."

"Why did he follow them today instead arresting them last night?" Clint asked.

"To tell you the truth," Eldred said, "I don't think he trusted me to back him up."

Clint could believe that. He certainly wouldn't have trusted the sheriff of Baskerville to watch his back in a fight.

But he knew the man was still lying about something.

"All right, Sheriff." He turned and walked to the door.

"You're leavin'?" Eldred could not keep the hopeful tone out of his voice.

"No," Clint said, "I'm going to take a look around town, first."

"What are you lookin' for?"

"Any indication that you're lying to me," Clint said. "If I find out you are, I'll be back."

The sheriff opened his mouth, but no sound came out. Before he could find his voice, Clint left.

Clint looked up and down the street. Baskerville was not a thriving town, but what few people there were seemed to be congregated down the street. He decided to go over and see what they were all so interested in.

When he reached them he found mostly men and a few women crowded around something.

"Somebody should get the sheriff," a man said.

"What good would he do?" a woman's voice asked, disdainfully.

"Excuse me," Clint said. "What are we looking at here?"

A couple of men turned and looked at him, then stepped apart and said, "Take a look, friend. It ain't a pretty sight."

Clint moved forward and found that they were all standing around a horse trough. In the trough, having floated to the top, was the body of a man who did not seem to have a face. Someone had shot it off, and made a half-hearted attempt at submerging the body in the trough. Whatever they had used to weigh it down obviously had not worked.

"I wonder who he is?"

Clint reached down and took a badge out of the dead man's shirt pocket that had the words MARSHAL and ABILENE on it.

"I know who he is," he said. He turned and started back to the sheriff's office.

THIRTY-FOUR

When Clint entered the sheriff's office the door slammed back against the wall and threatened to come off its hinges. The sheriff cringed behind his desk, apparently feeling flight would have been futile. On the desk was his gunbelt and gun. As Clint came closer he backed away until his back was to the wall. He put his hands up helplessly.

Clint came around the desk, grabbed the man by the front of the shirt and began banging him against the wall. A gun rack which had been precariously perched fell off the wall, sending rifles and shotguns everywhere. Still, Clint slammed the man against the wall and continued to do so until he was too exhausted to go on. When he released him the sheriff slid to the floor and laid there, his hands still held in front of him in a futile effort at warding off Clint's anger, more than the physical violence.

"You're a poor excuse for a lawman!" Clint shouted.

"I know, I know," the man blubbered, "but I didn't know . . ."

"Didn't know what?"

"That they were gonna kill him."

Clint kicked the man once and asked, "Would it have mattered if you did know?"

"I don't know, I don't know . . . I was afraid . . ."

Clint didn't know if the man was truly afraid, got paid off, or both.

"Where did they go?"

"I don't know!" Eldred shouted. "They really did leave this mornin'."

"How long ago?"

"About six hours."

"Which way did they ride?"

"West."

Clint was amazed that he was that close, considering what had gone on during the past couple of days. None of the action had gotten very far from Abilene.

Clint bent over and grabbed the badge on the man's shirt. He tore it off, taking a good chunk of the shirt with it.

"Don't . . ." the sheriff sobbed, "don't . . ."

Clint leaned over and held the badge in front of the blubbering man's face.

"If I ever hear that you're wearing this again, I'll come back and kill you. Do you understand?"

"Yes, yes . . ."

"You are going to collect the marshal's body and have it ready to be transported back to Abilene by the time I get back."

"W-when will you be back?"

"I don't know!" Clint shouted. "But it better be ready when I get here."

"It'll be ready," the now ex-sheriff said.

"It better be."

Clint threw the badge across the room, turned and left. Outside he mounted up and started west.

THIRTY-FIVE

Mike Paul and Ray Hogan had never been so happy in their lives. They were in a whorehouse in Decatur, Kansas, a town where, in a few hours time, they had already spent more money than either of them had ever seen, and been with more women than either of them had ever been with.

At the moment they had two whores in their hotel room—the fifth and sixth they had bought themselves time with—and were each using one on a separate bed. Paul had a big-busted blonde on her hands and knees and was gleefully taking her from behind. She was whooping and hollering as he pounded into her, telling him that he was the biggest and best she had ever been with. Once she saw how much money he had she'd decided to tell him everything he'd ever wanted to hear about being a man.

On the other bed Hogan was lying on his back with a brunette crouched between his legs. She was tall and slender, with small, taut breasts, the nipples of which she kept rubbing over his thighs because he was so hairy it felt good. She had the thumb and forefinger of her right hand around the base of his penis, which was long and rather skinny, she thought. She was working his cock in and out of her mouth, wetting it thoroughly, licking the head and then driving her head down over it so she could engulf it quickly, and then sucking her way back up to the spongy head again. Her name was Vivian and her blonde friend's name was Lola. Lola had complained to her that the man she was with—Mike Paul—stank, had a small penis and was not very good. Vivian, for the money she was being paid, could put up with the smell that was coming from Hogan—after all, he *was* a man—and decided that she had gotten the best part of the deal because he did have a long and rather interesting penis, and he seemed to know how to use it. Lola wanted to switch off at some point, and Vivian was considering it because they were such good friends.

At the moment though they were both rather involved. The air was filled with the sound of moist flesh slapping flesh, Lola was hollering at her man, lying to him about how good he was and Vivian's man was moaning and grunting as she brought him closer and closer to shooting his load.

Neither man realized that the money trail they had left over the past few hours was much clearer than any trail they had left in the dirt.

Damien rode into Decatur, pleased to find that he had been correct. The two men had indeed met up and he had followed their combined trail here rather easily. Once in town, it wasn't hard to find their money trail. In the saloon he heard men talking about the two crazy cowboys in the hotel who were using whores like they were going out of style, after they had gone on a spending spree in the saloon and the general store.

"Don't know where they got at all that money," one man standing at the bar said, "but it couldn'ta been honest and they's fools to be spendin' it the way they are."

"Yeah," another man said, "you wish you had that much money to throw around on whores."

"They're in the hotel, you say?" Damien asked.

"That's right," the first man said.

"Which hotel would that be?"

"Onliest one we got," the second man said.

"Much obliged," Damien said, and left the saloon.

He considered stopping first at the sheriff's office, but decided against it. He worked better alone. He'd bring the lawman in on it afterward.

He walked down to the hotel and as soon as he entered the lobby he could hear voices, both men and women, hooting and hollering. The desk clerk had the good sense to look embarrassed by it all.

"That been goin' on long?" Damien asked.

"Coupla hours," the clerk said. "Different whores goin' in and out. Them two cowboys can sure go awhile."

"Not much longer," Damien said under his breath, and started up the stairs.

THIRTY-SIX

Outside of Baskerville Clint found the next body. He was tired of finding bodies left behind by Ralph Markus.

He dismounted and walked over to the body. Off in a nearby clearing a saddle mount stood unconcernedly as he bent over the fallen man. He was young, younger than Markus had been, but not by much. Obviously, Markus had decided to leave one of his boys behind.

Clint ran down the horse on foot and saw that there were no saddlebags. The reason Markus had killed him was obviously for his share of the money. He also had an extra gun, since the young man's gunbelt was missing.

First Alex McCord, then Joe Bags and now this fella. When Clint Adams found Ralph Markus he was going to make sure that the Abilene bank robbery was the last bank job he ever pulled.

Damien stopped outside the room where all the commotion was coming from. From the sound of it the men were still very involved with the whores. Damien held a knife in each hand. He backed away from the door, lifted his foot and kicked out as hard as he could. His heel hit the door just above the doorknob and it snapped open, slamming into the inside wall.

As he stepped in he saw lots of skin. One man was crouched behind a blonde with a big, pale butt while another woman was crouched over a man so that Damien had a good look at her smaller, firmer—and much more to his taste—butt.

The women screamed, a different kind of scream than before. The men stared at him, one from over his shoulder as he was still engaged with the blonde, and the other from beneath the dark-haired girl.

"Let's don't anybody make any sudden moves," he said.

At that both men leaped for their guns, hanging on their respective bedposts. Since Damien only had the two knives he didn't have a choice in the matter. You did not throw a "warning knife," in this situation.

He let both knives fly, and they struck their targets with a wet thud. One man fell over with a knife sticking out of his back, while the other clutched at the one that was protruding from his side. The whores ran screaming and naked from the room, the blonde's big tits bouncing and flopping about. Damien really did prefer the dark-haired girl's slender body. He couldn't think about that now, however. He was going to have a lot of explaining to do to another lawman, very shortly.

THIRTY-SEVEN

The sheriff of Decatur came in and unlocked Damien's cell.

"Well, I checked your story with Abilene," he said, as he swung the cell door open. "It checks out."

"Thanks."

"Come into the office and I'll give you back your knives."

They went into the office and stood on their own sides of the lawman's desk. On it sat Damien's knives. The last time he had seen them they were imbedded in bank robbers.

"Are they both dead?" he asked.

"Yep. You want 'em?"

"What for?"

"To take 'em back."

"I'll just take back the money."

The sheriff didn't speak. He was a potbellied man in his fifties who looked as if he'd been wearing his badge a long time. It was both tarnished and dented.

"You do have the money from the bank robbery, don't you?" Damien asked him.

The sheriff sighed, bent down and came up with two sets of saddlebags from beneath his desk. He dropped them on top.

"It's all there," he said, "minus whatever they spent in town."

"They were only here a few hours," Damien said. "How much could they have spent?"

"I don't know," the sheriff said, "but they were trying."

Damien picked up his knives, put one in his belt sheath and simply tucked the other into his belt, then picked up the saddlebags. They each felt lighter than the one he'd gotten from the Mexican.

"What's wrong?" the lawman asked.

"Seems they did spend some," Damien said.

"I told you they did. Why?"

"They feel lighter."

"Lighter?"

"Than the one I got from one of the other thieves."

The lawman squinted at him.

"How do I know you'll really take the money back to Abilene?" he asked, going on the offensive.

"You don't," Damien said, "just as I don't know how much you might have took out for yourself."

"Now wait a minute—"

"It don't matter to me, Sheriff," Damien said, quickly. "The bank's gonna be happy to get back however much they get. If you felt entitled—"

"I think you better get out of my office and out of my town, mister," the sheriff said, indignantly.

"I'm gettin', Sheriff," Damien said, "I'm gettin'."

• • •

It took longer this time to get back to the point where they picked up all the trails. Now the trail Clint was following was the clearest and Damien didn't have to be very good at tracking at all to follow it. Weighed down with three saddlebags of money he decided to start following it until he either caught up with Clint, or met him coming back.

Very briefly the thought occurred to him that he was now in possession of more money than he'd ever had before, more money than he'd ever even seen before. What was to stop him from picking another direction and just going? After all, when Clint didn't find him what would he assume? That he'd stolen the money, or that he'd caught up with one of the bank robbers who had killed him?

But it didn't matter what Clint thought. What mattered was what Damien thought, and taking off with money that wasn't his—and that men had died for—was just not something that he wanted to do.

He started following Clint's trail.

THIRTY-EIGHT

Ralph Markus rode for a week, stopping only to pick up the most meager of supplies, and eventually came to a stop in a town called Cheyenne Wells, in Colorado. He'd felt the need to put some miles between him and Abilene, and also to get out of Kansas.

Cheyenne Wells was not a large town, but it would suit his needs. He needed a couple of days' worth of rest and the town had all he needed; a livery, a hotel, a saloon. Later he'd find out if it had decent food and women, but for now what he saw suited him.

He took his horse to the livery and gave it over to the liveryman there. When the man started to reach for his saddlebags Markus shouted, "No!" and grabbed them first.

"Sorry," he said. "I just don't like people touchin' my things."

"Sure, mister," the liveryman said, "sure. Whatever you say."

Markus also removed his rifle from the saddle, leaving

the liveryman behind shaking his head at how crazy some people acted.

Markus registered in the hotel and locked himself in his room. At one point he'd transferred Lonnie Field's share of the money into his own saddlebags so that he wouldn't have two sets of bags on his horse. That would have looked curious to the liveryman.

He upended the saddlebags and dumped the money on the bed. He had over eight thousand dollars there, and what was he going to do with it? If he walked around town carrying his saddlebags some saddle tramp and his partner would decide he had something of value in there. On the other hand, he couldn't just leave it in the hotel room, unless he hid it real good. A cursory examination of the room, sparely furnished, told him that wasn't a possibility.

If he was in a town where he was going to stay a while, like someplace in California, he could simply put the money in the bank. That would be ironic, since he had stolen the money *from* a bank, but it sure would have been safer than leaving it in the hotel or carrying it with him.

Still, if he did that in a small town word would get around. He didn't need that.

He was stuck. The bills were twenties and hundreds, nothing bigger, so there was a lot of them. He could put a thousand dollars in hundreds in each boot . . . He sat down to think about this. A thousand in each boot, and then some in his pockets . . . wait . . . maybe he could work this out.

By the time he was done he had money in his boots, in the legs of his trousers, inside his shirt, in his shirt pocket, his trouser pockets and inside his hat. It scraped him a bit inside the legs of his trousers and his torso, but he could put up with that. He had his trousers tucked into his boots, and his shirt tucked into his pants, so there was no danger of the money coming out. It could move around in there all it wanted.

The money in his shirt pocket was enough for his expenses—food, drinks, gambling or women—but not enough to attract attention. If he did end up with a woman he'd have her meet him back here so he'd have time to undress and put the money back in his saddlebags.

When he was satisfied that no one would be able to tell by looking at him that he had over eight thousand dollars on him he decided he was ready to leave the room and get some food.

He walked down the hall to the stairs and then down to the lobby. He felt the money moving around, but that was okay. It was also making some noise, but only he could hear it. By the time he reached the front door he was pleased with the outcome and very happy to have thousands of dollars rubbing up against his bare skin, as well as in his boots. He knew that rich men carried their money in fat leather wallets, but that wasn't for him.

This was what having money was all about.

THIRTY-NINE

Clint had to call on all his dubious skills as a tracker once Markus left Baskerville, because now it was one man on one horse and he was alone tracking him. Several times he thought he had lost the trail only to pick it up again, one time doubling back to find it. Each time he found the trail again he felt he had fallen farther and farther behind.

On a couple of occasions he came to a small town or a trading post and was able to determine that Markus had been there and purchased supplies. His best guess was that although he had started out about six or eight hours behind him, he was now at least a full day behind. This would certainly have not happened if Damien was with him.

Clint wondered how Damien had done in finding the other two bank robbers. Surely, after a week, he must have found both of them while Clint was still hopelessly trailing Ralph Markus.

However, he would trail him for a week, a month, even a year if he had to. The deaths of Alex McCord and Joe Bags would certainly not go unpunished, not to mention the murder of Markus's own man. A man like that would surely kill again when the need arose. Clint only hoped he would catch him before that happened.

Damien picked up Clint's trail easily enough and followed it to Baskerville, where he found a town without a sheriff.

"Damndest thing," the liveryman told him. "He just up and left town."

"What happened?"

"Well, we had us a killin'."

"Who got killed?"

The old man leaned in close and said, "The marshal of Abilene. Seems he was huntin' some bank robbers and they ended up here."

"And what happened?" Damien asked. Instinctively, he knew that this man knew everything that had gone on.

"Well, sir," the man said, "you ain't gonna believe this, but the Gunsmith hisself was here."

"I believe it, old timer," Damien said. "Just tell me what happened and don't leave anything out."

After the liveryman had given him the whole story Damien went to the undertaker, where he found Joe Bags waiting in a box for Clint to return.

"And he's gettin' ripe," the undertaker said. "I don't know what to do, mister. The sheriff—the ex-sheriff, that is—said that if I didn't have this body ready to travel when the Gunsmith got back that he was gonna kill me. And then the sheriff, he left town!"

The undertaker was obviously afraid that Clint Adams was going to come back and kill him.

"Don't worry," Damien said. "You're not gonna get killed. Here's what I want you to do. Bury the marshal in a plain pine box."

"B-but, who's gonna pay?"

"I'll pay."

"And what do I tell Clint Adams when he gets back?"

"You let me worry about Clint Adams," Damien said. "He's a friend of mine. I'm gonna find him and I'll be comin' back this way with him, so he's not gonna kill you."

"Really?"

"I guarantee it."

The undertaker heaved a sigh of relief.

"Mister," he said, "you're a life saver."

"Yeah, well," Damien said, "maybe I am. You just get the marshal here buried nice and proper for me."

"Yes, sir."

Damien knew he was a few days behind Clint Adams by the time he left Baskerville. He also knew that Clint had no idea how long he'd be on Ralph Markus's trail, which was why he told the sheriff to have the body of the marshal ready. If he knew it was going to take him this long he never would have asked that. The last thing he wanted was his friend's body rotting above ground.

Outside of town he found the body of Lonnie Fields. He figured the body for the thief who'd been riding with Markus. But he couldn't figure who killed him, Clint or Markus himself. Chances were better that the thieves had fallen out and Markus had killed the man for his share. The body was without its gunbelt, and his horse was long gone. Damien just had the feeling that this wasn't the work of Clint Adams, no matter how grieved he was over the death of Joe Bags. If it had been Markus's body, that would have been different.

They'd started this hunt out with vengeance in the eye of the marshal, and now he was sure it was in the eyes of Clint Adams. It must have been a serious blow to him to see his friend floating in the horse trough. Damien sure wouldn't want to be Ralph Markus when Clint caught up with him.

FORTY

Ralph Markus had himself a good meal in a restaurant he found down the street from the hotel. The money chafed him as he sat and people eating around him must have thought he had some kind of a rash, the way he was scratching and fidgeting. Markus didn't notice them at all.

After he left the restaurant he went to the saloon, where he had a drink in more comfort because he was able to stand at the bar. As the night wore on the saloon girls appeared and he soon picked out one in particular he liked. She was a big-bosomed blonde who reminded him of Dixie, from Abilene. Only this one had a sweet face and a kind smile, and after talking to her for half the night he felt sure that she would never treat him the way Dixie did. As he got drunker and drunker he managed to convince himself that this was the girl of his dreams. Finally he convinced her to come to his hotel room when she was done working, by leaving a twenty-dollar bill in her cleavage. Then he went back to his room to get all of the money out of his shirt and pants and back into the saddlebags before she showed up.

Only before she got there he fell asleep on the bed, fully dressed, money and all.

It was the knocking on the door that woke Markus. He sat up and looked around, realized that he'd fallen asleep with all the money still on him, boots and all.

"Wait!" he shouted.

"Hey," she said from outside, "you asked me to come, remember?"

"Just wait a minute."

He starting pulling money out of his shirt, but he had started sweating while he was asleep and the paper was sticking to his skin. He pulled off his boots and frantically took the money out of them and stuffed it into the saddlebags. He finally got all the money that was stuck to his back and chest off and into the saddlebags, as well.

"Hello?" she said, knocking again.

He looked around. Now he only had money in his pants and maybe he'd be able to get them off without her seeing it. He went to the door and opened it for her. She stood in the hall, looking at him curiously.

"Are you all right?" she asked.

"I'm fine."

"You look . . . funny."

"I—I fell asleep."

"Well, it's no wonder," she said, coming in, "the way you were drinkin' before."

He closed the door and said, "I was, uh, celebratin'."

"Celebratin' what?"

He ran his hand over his face, and then said, "Uh, meetin' you."

"Ooh, how sweet," she said. "All right, you're forgiven for makin' me wait in the hall."

"Look, uh, I'm just gonna put some water on my face," he said. "Make yourself comfortable."

She smiled, dropped the shawl she was wearing and said, "Okay." Her cleavage was impressive—not as impressive as Dixie's had been. This girl was not quite as big as Dixie, but she was big enough.

As he washed his face and hands using the pitcher and basin on the dresser the girl removed her dress and underwear and stood there waiting for him to turn around. When he did she sucked in her tummy and stuck out her breasts because she knew that was a pose men liked. This one was kind of odd, but she had the feeling he had money, and he wasn't bad looking. She'd fucked worse for a lot less than she'd already gotten from this one.

"Well?" she asked.

He stared at her naked body. Her breasts were round and firm, the nipples pink like Dixie's. Elsewhere, though, she was kind of skinny, not like Dixie at all. He wondered why earlier he'd been thinking of her as his dream girl. She had a nice set of tits and a pretty face, but her arms and legs were kind of skinny and when she did a slow turn for him she didn't have much of a butt.

He was disappointed, and it showed.

"Whatsa matter?" she asked. "You don't like what you see?"

"Well . . . uh, no, not really. I mean, you look nice, but . . ."

"But what?" she asked. "Hey, you paid me twenty bucks to come up here, friend. Am I wastin' my time here?"

"Um," he said, drying his still wet palms on his pants, "I think you better get dressed and go."

He wasn't feeling well, anyway. Being awakened that abruptly, and all the drinking, he just didn't feel like having a girl with him tonight—not this one, anyway.

"Son-of-a-bitch," she was muttering as she got dressed, "I had better offers tonight, you know, from real men!"

"What?"

She glared at him.

"I got real men who want me tonight," she said, "not some limp dick like you."

She grabbed her shawl and started for the door but he intercepted her and grabbed her by the hair.

"H-hey!" she cried out in pain.

"What did you call me?" he demanded, hotly.

"I d-didn't call you nothin' " she said. "Let go!"

"Not until you repeat what you said!"

"Limp dick!" she shouted back. "I called you a limp dick—now let me go!"

Instead of letting her go, though, he turned her around and grabbed her by the throat. She gagged as his hands closed around her neck and he started to squeeze.

"That . . . wasn't . . . nice," he said.

FORTY-ONE

Although Eclipse was still not a greatly experienced trail horse Clint decided to ride all night. By the light of the moon he managed to stay on the trail and when daybreak came and the trail became clearer he breathed a sigh of relief that he'd been following the right one. If he'd managed to lose it during the night and had picked up another one by mistake then all the night riding would have been wasted. He would have felt stupid not only for wasting time, but for risking injury to his horse for no reason.

When he saw that there was a town up ahead, he felt even better. Whether or not Markus had stopped there he could at least have himself a decent meal before continuing on.

As he rode into town he passed a signpost that said Cheyenne Wells, Colorado.

During the night he'd crossed the border from Kansas to Colorado without even realizing it.

• • •

As he rode into town there was some commotion going on and he had a bad, bad feeling about it. It reminded him of the atmosphere when Joe Bags had been found floating in the horse trough back in Baskerville.

As he approached the center of town he saw that most of the people in the street were gathered in front of the hotel. He tied Eclipse off across the street, away from the action, and walked across.

"What's going on?" he asked somebody.

A man turned to him and said, "They found a dead woman in the hotel."

"A stranger?"

"No," someone else said, "one of the saloon girls." '

"How was she killed?"

"We don't know," the man said. "All we heard was that she was dead, found in one of the rooms."

"Where's your sheriff?"

"Inside."

At this point, of course, Clint still didn't know about the saloon girl, Dixie, being killed back in Abilene. But the mere fact that there had been a killing gave him cause to want to talk to the sheriff.

He made his way to the front of the crowd and into the hotel lobby.

"Hey, mister," a deputy said, "you can't come in here."

"I'd like to see you sheriff."

"Yeah, well, we're a little busy, at the moment," the deputy said. "Had us a killing here last night."

"That's what I want to see him about," Clint said. "I might have some information."

The deputy squinted at him suspiciously and Clint noticed the man's hand hovering near his gun.

"Whataya mean information?"

"My name is Clint Adams," Clint said. "I'm tracking a bank robber from Abilene who killed a deputy and a marshal, and one of his own men."

"And you tracked him here?"

"That's right."

"And you think he did this?"

"I think maybe he did," Clint said. "If I could compare notes with your sheriff maybe we could figure it out."

The man thought a moment, then said, "All right, come with me."

There was a small crowd in the lobby, probably mostly guests and hotel employees. They worked their way through them and then Clint followed the deputy up the stairs to the second floor. They walked down a hall to a room with a few people outside, including the sheriff and a man who looked like he might be the hotel manager.

"Sheriff?" the deputy said.

The sheriff looked up and frowned. He was an older man, in his fifties, while the deputy was in his thirties.

"Bates, I thought I told you to stay downstairs and keep people out. Who's this?"

"Sheriff, this fella says he might know somethin'," the deputy said. "I thought I should bring him up. He says—"

"All right, I'll hear what he has to say," the sheriff said. "You go back downstairs."

"Yes, sir."

As the deputy walked away the sheriff asked, "How long have you been in town?"

"Just rode in."

"So what makes you think you know something about this?"

"My name is Clint Adams, Sheriff," Clint said. "I've

been tracking some bank robbers from Abilene for about the last ten days."

"Abilene? I heard about that. You're Adams, huh? The Gunsmith?"

"That's right?"

"Wearin' a badge?"

"No," Clint said, "but I've got one." Clint dug Joe Bags's marshal of Abilene badge out of his pocket and showed it to the man.

"What are you doin' with that?"

"The man I'm tracking killed the marshal," Clint said.

"What's your interest?"

"He was a friend of mine," Clint said. "I was riding with his posse."

"And where's the rest of the posse?"

"Most of them were storekeepers," Clint said. "They turned around and went back after a day."

The sheriff made a face like he tasted something bad and said, "That figures. All right, you want to take a look?"

"Sure."

The sheriff waved him on. Clint stepped forward and looked in the room. The woman was sprawled half on the bed and half off, her head hanging so he could see the red, raw marks on her throat.

"Strangled her?"

"That's right."

"My man killed a deputy in Abilene, then the marshal when he tracked him to a town called Baskerville. Outside of Baskerville he killed one of his own men."

"Shot them all?"

"Yes."

"Why would you think he did this?"

"I don't know that he did," Clint said. "I don't know

that it's my man, but if it is, he's starting to kill more often." Clint looked at the sheriff. "What name did he register under?"

The sheriff looked at the other men, who turned out to be the manager, as Clint had thought.

"Smith," the man said.

"Can I go inside?" Clint asked.

"Sure."

Clint entered the room and got a better look at the woman. Blonde, she must have been pretty, and she had been well endowed. Her clothes had been torn off her, either before or after she was strangled. Clint looked around the room and was about to leave when he saw the edge of something under the bed. He leaned over and picked it up, carried it to the door.

"What've you got there?" the sheriff asked.

Clint showed it to him. It was a hundred dollar bill.

"I'm going to assume a lot of cowboys around here don't carry hundred dollar bills."

"But a man who had recently robbed a bank would."

"You got a telegraph office?" Clint asked. "I want to send a telegram to Abilene."

"Sure thing," the sheriff said. "Come with me."

When they got an answer back from Abilene Clint read it and turned to look at the sheriff.

"After we left Abilene a woman was found dead in the hotel."

"Strangled?"

He nodded and said, "And naked. Also blonde and big."

"Found in whose room?"

"A man named Ralph Markus."

"The man you're lookin' for?"

"Yep."

The sheriff sighed. "Then it looks like this was your man."

"Yep," Clint said, "looks like it."

FORTY-TWO

The deputy brought Clint's horse to the front of the sheriff's office, where Clint and the sheriff—whose name was Fulton—were standing on the boardwalk talking.

"Nearest we can figure from the hotel clerk and the liveryman," Fulton said, "he musta left about two hours ago."

"That's the closest I've been to him in a while," Clint said. "I better get a move on."

"You okay?" Fulton asked. "You look likc you rode all night."

"I did," Clint said, "which is the only reason I'm this close."

"Well," Fulton said, "that's a mighty fine lookin' horse, Mr. Adams, but even he's gotta rest some time."

"After we catch him," Clint said, taking the reins from the deputy, "we'll both rest."

As he mounted up the sheriff asked, "So you just gonna keep on trailin' him?"

Clint sat in the saddle and looked down at the lawman.

"I'm through trailing him, Sheriff."

"So what are you gonna do?"

"Me and Eclipse, here," Clint said, patting the big Arabian's neck, "we're just going to run him to ground."

Markus had tried to sneak out of town but he couldn't really make it without at least the liveryman seeing him. Of course, he could have killed the man, but he wasn't angry enough—which was when he killed women—and couldn't really see the profit in it—which was when he killed men. So he just took his horse and lit out of there, hoping it would be hours before anyone found the dead saloon girl in his hotel room.

Of course, it was the girl's own fault she was dead. He never took the blame for that. If they'd behave in a proper way they wouldn't get killed, would they? If they'd act like ladies—but how could you expect saloon girls and whores to act like ladies? He decided that when he did reach California he was going to go straight to San Francisco, where all the women were ladies. He'd get himself some proper clothes, become a proper gentleman, and would only take up with proper ladies—the kind who wouldn't care how big he was as long as he had plenty of money and manners.

All he'd have to do was learn some manners.

Clint rode Eclipse hard, following the trail left by Ralph Markus and his horse. By now he knew the tracks of the horse well. There was nothing so odd about them, but after tracking them so long they had become distinctive.

He now had to add the saloon girl from Abilene and the saloon girl from Cheyenne Wells to the list of people Markus had killed. And who knew how many other women and men he'd left dead behind him? Funny, but if someone had found the girl in Abilene sooner, maybe this could all have been avoided. They could have arrested him there and then for the killing of that girl and put him away. The rest of his gang probably would have disbanded and drifted away. Now there was only one way Clint could see to stop Markus, once and for all.

He was tired, and he knew Eclipse was tired, but you wouldn't have known it from the way the big Arabian was moving. Even if Markus was moving at a gallop his horse couldn't possibly have been going as fast as Eclipse. Sooner or later they'd have to catch up to him, or collapse.

Clint hoped it was sooner.

Damien could tell by Clint's tracks that he was well behind him. Also, he hadn't come across a campfire of any kind, so it appeared as of Clint had ridden all night.

Damien had stopped for the night, though, and he was sitting with a cup of coffee thinking about the events of the past ten days or see. He'd killed three men in that time, and had in his possession well over ten thousand dollars. That was a lot of money to be sitting out on the prairie with, with nobody else around to know that you have it.

He pulled the three sets of saddlebags over and decided to try and consolidate them. He took the money out of two of them and started stuffing it all into the third set. As he did so he stopped every so often to examine a twenty-dollar bill, or a fifty, or a hundred. He'd seen twenties before, but fifties and hundreds, they were kind of new to him.

That sheriff in Decatur. He'd helped himself to some of the money, Damien was sure. How much? A hundred? Maybe a thousand? Figuring who'd miss it? And who would? Damien sure didn't know how much had been taken from the bank overall. It seemed to him from the saddlebags he'd recovered that each man's share had come to maybe three or four thousand. So maybe they took between eighteen and twenty-four thousand from the bank, without ever having opened the safe?

He finished packing all of the bills into one set of saddlebags and wondered how much they would have gotten if they had gotten into the safe.

FORTY-THREE

In the distance there was a rider. But so small he couldn't be made out. And yet who else could it have been? There was open ground between them, and they were the only two around. There was only the distance between them that was keeping this thing from ending.

It would end today, one way or another.

And off in the distance a second rider, too far away to make out, but coming with great determination astride a powerful horse who was gobbling up the ground with every stride. Both were tired, neither would let up until they had reached their common goal.

Ralph Markus didn't know what to do. Instinctively he knew this was the Gunsmith coming after him. Why had the man taken it upon himself to catch him? What had he ever done to him? Markus knew he could not take the Gunsmith, not alone, and with no one around to posture for he gave in to his fear and it etched itself on his face.

Clint Adams was coming and coming fast, and what could he do but run?

Clint could see the distance between himself and Ralph Markus decreasing by the minute. Before long the man was in range but he did not remove his gun. He intended to literally run the man to ground.

Markus wondered why there were no shots being fired. God, he could hear the Gunsmith's horse's hooves striking the ground, hear the way it was heaving from its nostrils.

What was he waiting for?"

Clint could see the fear on Markus's face every time the man looked over his shoulder at him. And then it happened. Although the man was riding the fresher mount it was his horse who took a bad step and went down. Markus went over the horse's head and landed hard on his back. Clint could hear the sound the man's body made when it struck the ground, and the sound of the air being slammed from his lungs.

Since Markus was going nowhere Clint took the time to ride after the man's horse, capture and bring it back. He dismounted, then, and checked the contents of the man's saddlebags. Satisfied that he had all of Markus's share of the money he tossed the saddlebags onto his own horse, then walked to the fallen man.

"H-help," Markus said. "H-help me. I c-can't move."

He looked down at Ralph Markus, killer of women, lawmen and partners, and saw the pain on the man's face.

"Can't move?" Clint asked.

"I c-can't move, and I c-can't feel anything—can't feel my legs or my arms."

"Hmm," Clint said, standing where the man could see him, "sounds like you've got a broken back."

He knew the man wasn't faking. He'd heard the sound he'd made when he hit the ground. But to be sure he crouched next to Markus and poked and prodded him with no result.

"Yep," Clint said, "you got a broken back, all right."

"You gotta help me," Markus said. "Y-you gotta get me to a doctor."

"There's nothing a doctor can do for you, son," Clint said. "Can't fix a broken back."

"You mean . . . I got to stay like this?"

"For the rest of you life."

"B-but I can't!"

"I wish you luck," Clint said, standing up, all desire to kill the man gone now. He was already as good as dead.

"Wait a minute," Markus said. "You can't leave me like this."

"Sure I can," Clint said. "You'll either starve to death, or some predator will come along and finish you."

"P-predator?"

"Sure," Clint said. "A buzzard, a fox, maybe a wolf or a big cat," Clint said. "Something will come along and put you out of your misery soon enough."

"Wait, wait . . ." Markus said, panicked as Clint disappeared from his line of vision. "Adams, you got to finish me. You can't leave me like this."

Clint walked to his horse and mounted up. He then rode over to Markus so he could look down at the man one last time.

"I killed the marshal," Markus said. "I—I killed the deputy, and some women—"

"I know all about it, Markus."

"Then finish me. Kill me. I know you want to."

"You're right," Clint said. "I did want to, but not anymore. I'm just going to leave you here and let you die. I hope the buzzards come down first, too, because they'll go for the eyes first. Pluck them right out of your head and eat them."

"No!" Markus shrieked. "No, no!"

"Good-bye, Markus," Clint said, and turned his horse away from the man.

As he rode away he could hear Markus screaming for a long time, and he savored every moment of it.

FORTY-FOUR

When Clint rode into Abilene he was immediately spotted and the word spread. By the time he got to the bank the manager, Gerald Hawkins, was waiting out front.

"Did you get it?" Hawkins asked. "Did you get the money back?"

Clint stared down at the manager. He could have tossed him the saddlebags he had, which contained probably half what was taken, but he didn't.

"Did anyone else come back?" Clint asked.

"Well, the day after you left—"

"I mean, after that," Clint said.

"Well . . . the marshal didn't come back, if that's what—"

"He's dead."

"Oh."

"What about Damien?"

"Damien? I don't—"

"The man we were using as a tracker."

"Another man did come back a couple of days ago."

"Did he give you anything?"

"No, he didn't even stop here."

"Is he still in town?"

"As far as I know."

Clint decided to check the hotel and the saloon for Damien. He knew the man had some of the money when they separated, and if he found the other two bank robbers than he had their shares, as well.

"Mr. Adams," Hawkins said. "Did you get the money?"

"I'll be back to talk to you later, Mr. Hawkins."

He turned his horse and ignored the protests of the bank manager. As he rode past the general store a man in an apron came running out to him. He recognized him as one of the posse who had turned back.

"Mr. Adams," the man said, "thank God you're back."

"What is it?"

"That fella, Damien? The tracker?"

"What about him?"

"Well, he got back a few days ago and he's just been sittin' in the saloon with some saddlebags on the table in front of him. Then at night he goes to the hotel, and then next day he goes back to the saloon."

"With the saddlebags?"

"Yes, sir."

"Is he there now?"

"Yes, sir, at the Long Branch."

"I'll take care of it, mister . . ." Clint didn't remember the man's name and rode off before the man could remind him.

Clint entered the Long Branch with his saddlebags full of money. He saw Damien sitting at a far table, just as the storekeeper had said, with saddlebags on the table, and a beer.

"Beer," he told the bartender.

The bartender brought it and said, "He jest sits there with them saddlebags."

Clint ignored the bartender, walked over to the table, dropped his two sets of saddlebags on the table next to Damien's and sat down.

"Damien."

"You get 'im? Markus?"

"I got him. The rest?"

"I got 'em."

"Good."

They sipped their beers.

"Lots of money in these saddlebags, Clint."

"You been thinking about that for two days, Damien?" Clint asked. "Since you got back?"

"Since before then," Damien said. "Money never held no fascination for me, Clint, but then I never seen this much."

"It belongs to the bank, Damien," Clint said. "To the people in the town who put it in the bank."

"We got it back."

"I know that."

"We risked our lives."

"I know that, too," Clint said, "but Joe Bags lost his life, Damien. To do what you're thinking of doing . . . well, I just wouldn't be able to go along with it."

Damien remained silent. Like Clint he had a week's growth of stubble on his face, as he hadn't bothered to shave—or bathe, apparently—since he got back.

"Damien?" Clint said. "Do you understand what I'm saying?"

Damien stared at him, then put his hand on top of the saddlebags and pushed them over toward Clint.

"Take 'em to the bank, Clint."

Clint leaned forward.

"There's nothing wrong with thinking what you were thinking, Damien," Clint said, "As long as we don't act on it."

"You were thinkin' it, too?"

"I was thinking that this is a lot of money."

Clint stood up and collected all the saddlebags.

"I'll return these to the bank and then I think I need a bath and a meal. What about you?"

Damien looked up at Clint and said, "I think I need to be on my way. I been around people too long."

"Don't you want to get some rest—"

"I got to get goin'," Damien said. "I ain't been thinkin' straight. Got to get off by myself."

"I understand," Clint said. "I'll be leaving soon myself."

"Ain't been thinkin' straight," Damien said, again.

"I know," Clint said. "Money does that to people."

"Not to me," Damien said. "Ain't never done nothin' to me . . . until now."

"You didn't do anything, Damien."

"But I thought about it," the man said, shaking his head. "That ain't like me, at all."

"Well," Clint said, hefting the saddlebags, "I better get these back. The bank manager's having kittens."

"You take it back," Damien said. "I'll be gone when you get back."

"See you again sometime, Damien," Clint said. "Much obliged for you coming along."

"Yeah," Damien said, "another time."

Clint left the saloon and walked over to the bank with the saddlebags of money.

Watch for

BULLETS FOR A BOY

232nd novel in the exciting GUNSMITH series
from Jove

Coming in April!